Home Comforts

Home Comforts

Bridie Costello

Matador
5 Weir Road
Kibworth Beauchamp
Leicester LE8 0LQ, UK
Tel: (+44) 116 279 2299
Fax: (+44) 116 279 2277
Email: books@troubador.co.uk
Web: www.troubador.co.uk/matador

ISBN 978 1848 764 415

British Library Cataloguing in Publication Data.
A catalogue record for this book is available from the British Library.

Typeset in 11pt Bembo by Troubador Publishing Ltd, Leicester, UK
Printed and bound in Great Britain by TJ International Ltd, Padstow, Cornwall

Matador is an imprint of Troubador Publishing Ltd

For my family

Chapter 1

Oh Lord, thought Stephen as he saw Tom approaching, he really didn't have time to make small talk to his new 'friend'; he was under pressure to finish a job and Tom didn't look too cheerful either. Tom was feeling just about as low as he could do; he wasn't cut out for this kind of life, and if something didn't turn up soon, well, he thought he might as well be dead. He couldn't deal with being homeless.

'How's it going there Tom, did you get a bed for yourself last night?' asked Stephen.

'I did, thanks for asking. The hostel gets filled early on cold nights.'

'I pity anyone who was sleeping out last night,' said Stephen as he looked at Tom with something akin to pity.

Although homeless, Tom looked after his appearance, he kept himself neat and tidy and Stephen thought that he looked less than his fifty years. Tom's brown hair was flecked with grey, he had dark eyes and he was quite handsome with an athletic looking body, he held himself erect and looked more than 5'11".

Stephen touched his own portly stomach and thought that he really should try to lose his beer belly, still his wife didn't complain. He had been married to Maura for twenty-three years now and Maura never complained. Maura said his receding hairline and chubby face were still beautiful to her and she loved his pale blue eyes, which seemed to twinkle when he smiled, at least that was what Maura said. In fact, Maura had never said anything of the sort; Stephen just hoped that she felt that way.

Stephen liked talking to Tom: it made him appreciate his own life even more and Tom was grateful for Stephen's concern. Stephen was a good sort and he often took the time to chat to Tom.

'Yes I did get a bed,' he repeated, 'but only just.'

'It's been a great day today, Tom and I've almost finished painting the old barracks at long last,' said Stephen looking up at his handiwork. 'It makes such a difference when you get the good weather Tom and I'm sure you like the fine weather as well.'

'I do like the outdoor life; I wouldn't mind doing your job. The fresh air and all are great but the nights spent outdoors are a killer, my chest can't take it.'

'I know Tom, I know. You would have liked doing the job on a day like today, there's no pressure when the weather is fine and I love being my own boss, that's a bonus. Do you know Tom I don't think I could ever work for someone else, I like only having myself, and of course the wife, to answer to.' Stephen wasn't going to tell Tom that he had no say in the business and that his wife ran the show, he was still living in the past; when he did have some control in 'his' company, as he liked to think of it.

'I envy you Stephen, I never got married, I never met the right person, maybe if I had I wouldn't be in this position now.'

'Ah now Tom, marriage isn't the be all and end all. Take today, I got up at six thirty and made tea for the missus before I had any myself, then I made a bit of breakfast for the two bucks and I had to call them three times before they got up. I'm telling you Tom teenagers can be a pain in the 'you know what', and all this before I load up the van and head in to the city trying to get in before traffic gets too heavy. There are drawbacks in the painting trade too; there are a lot of boring and fiddly jobs that have to be done. There's the cutting in, the undercoating, the glossing and the bloody brushes don't clean themselves! I'm telling you Tom the painting trade has its own drawbacks. Pricing jobs isn't a bowl of cherries either, Tom, you can come across some right awkward cusses.'

'Well right now I wish I had your problems Stephen.' Yes thought Tom, he wished he had Stephen's problems, and his life. Stephen didn't know when he was well off, he should count his blessings.

It had only been a few months since Tom's life had fallen apart, he'd owned his own company, his house and top of the range car and he'd lost the lot. He'd had a comfortable life but he'd become complacent and too trusting for his own good. Tom thought to himself how he had trusted everyone and anyone. Because I took my eye off the ball I've lost it all. Because my customers didn't pay me I couldn't pay my suppliers and my so called friendly bank manager wasn't so friendly any more. Oh he gave me a little leeway and a little pep talk but he didn't give me nearly enough time to try to get the money that was owed to me. A million euro never seemed that much, but when you try collecting it, it may as well be like climbing Mount Everest with your hands tied behind your back. Tom had to admit he had overstretched his finances during the last couple of years but who hadn't? After all the banks were throwing the money at him, even when he didn't want or need such big loans. I only needed to put my house up as collateral and the bank manager was my best buddy, thought Tom, you get a different sort of friend when they think you have money, fair weather friends the lot of them. Where are they when your money's gone? They're gone, as quick as they came. My friendly bank manager wasn't so friendly any more, in fact, he was never available to take my calls, and he dropped me like a hot potato.

Tom had met Mr Kenny, the aforementioned bank manager several times since becoming homeless, and he doesn't even acknowledge my existence, he looks straight through me, how quickly he forgot how good I was to him. I treated him to nights out at the dog track in Harold's Cross, I took him and his wife out to dinner on numerous occasions and this is how he repays me. Tom had even paid for a few weekends away for Mr and Mrs Kenny. I've only myself to blame, I got carried away, I thought I was in a different league. I was playing with the big boys but I didn't know how ruthless they could be. My construction company was doing alright to begin with, I just didn't keep enough control over it, and I'd always been too trusting. I'd always made sure that the insurance was up to date and it should have been more than sufficient to cover any unforeseen circumstances. That man, what was his name? Peter! Yes that was his name. Why was he working on site without a hard hat on? Why hadn't I checked that the insurance was paid? Why had I trusted the temp in the office? I should have realised that she would need some guidance for the first day or so, she wouldn't have been familiar with our computer system. I should have kept a tighter rein on the company's finances, so many regrets and if only, but why had I forgotten to make sure the insurance was paid up to date? How could I have forgotten something that important? Peter's family didn't want to hear my excuses or apologies, that wouldn't bring Peter back and it wouldn't put food on their table. I had ruined their lives as well as my own; I deserved to lose everything. The insurance company didn't care that I'd been with them for years, they didn't care that I'd lose my business or that Peter's family needed the compensation that was due to them. The insurance company didn't care full stop.

Stephen looked down his nose at Tom because he'd made a stupid mistake in business, but anyone can make mistakes. Stephen employed two or three men, maybe he would give Tom a job if he asked him for one, and he always said that he had too much work and not enough lads.

'Hey, Stephen I'm glad you're still here, there is something I want to ask you. Is there any chance of me getting a job in your painting business? I can use a paintbrush or do odd jobs for you, what do you say Stephen? I know you could use another man and I'm not afraid of hard work.'

'I don't know Tom, I have two lads working for me already, young lads don't expect big money straight off, and they're more interested in getting some experience behind them. They might not be the hardest workers but they do turn up, most of the time. I don't know Tom, let me think about it tonight and if you're around here tomorrow I'll let you know my answer then I can't promise you Tom, but I will give it some thought.'

'Jesus Stephen it's not rocket science and I'm not asking for top wages either, I'd take whatever you pay the other lads. Please Stephen, I'm not asking for a handout I just need someone to give me a break,' begged Tom.

'I know Tom, I didn't say no, but there are other things to consider and I can't give you an answer straight off.'

'What things? Stephen what have you got to consider?'

'Listen Tom, don't push me into a corner, I won't be pushed. I said I'd think about it and I will, now don't go on about it or the answer will be a definite no.'

'O.K, I'm sorry I won't rush you Stephen, I know you'll think about it, I just want to say I wouldn't let you down, I promise, I don't mean to go on at you. I'm desperate Stephen.'

'Go away now Tom, get yourself sorted with a bed for the night and get a good meal inside you. You've been looking a bit peaky the last few days; you need to take care of yourself.'

'I'm off now Stephen and thanks again for your concern and for not turning me down straight away about the job.'

'Ah Tom, I haven't said yes either, now be off and don't bother me anymore tonight.'

'O.K, goodnight Stephen, I'll see you first thing tomorrow.'

'Good luck Tom, good luck.'

If I have to keep begging him for a job, I will, thought Tom. I'm sure Stephen will give me a start tomorrow, why wouldn't he? He's a decent sort but I don't think he'll ever get 'Business Man of the Year' award, he's not driven enough and he certainly doesn't know the meaning of the word pressure. Still, I don't care as long as I can get back on the work scene, I wasn't cut out to be a bum and I'm not cut out for living rough on the streets; I'm too soft for that. I was too used to my home comforts and I hope to get used to them again with a bit of luck and some hard work. I suppose I'd better get back to Sheriff Street and see if I can get a bed again for the night, it will be a miracle if I do, most of the beds are taken by 7.30p.m. it must be getting on for 7.00p.m. by now. I'll never make it in time; it's at least another two miles to go. I miss not having a watch but I had to pawn it to get some money for food. I have to get a job and a room to bed down in soon, it's the middle of October, and I won't last the winter living the way I am now. Maybe I should have asked Stephen for a lift to the hostel, no, maybe not, that would have been pushing my luck. Almost there now, please let there be a bed for me.

I should have walked faster; the man in front of me got the last bed so it's up to the green for me, I won't be as slow tomorrow night. I could kick myself for missing out on a warm dry place to sleep; you're a fool Tom Dooley, a fool. Never mind, I'll wear both pairs of socks and my good old Aran sweater along with my old Cromby, and topped off with my sleeping bag I shall be as warm as toast. If I get the job with Stephen the first thing I'll buy for myself is a new pair of shoes, these old ones are letting in the water and it's hard to keep warm when your feet get damp. Ah good, the old bench is empty, I might get a nap in before the love birds start their canoodling after the pubs close, oh to be young again. Jesus, they're noisy tonight, I was just having a nice dream, I can't remember what I was dreaming about but I'm sure it was nice. I can't believe how young some of these lovebirds are, I don't think they're old enough to be doing what they do. I know it must be after closing time for the pubs, and these kids will be here for another hour or so. If their parents knew half of what they get up to they wouldn't let them out at night, the young ones today don't care what they do, or where they do it. Their attitude is all wrong, they've no respect for themselves or anyone else, I'd better forget about them and try to get back to sleep, I need to be at my best in the morning. If Stephen's decided to give me the job I don't want him to think he's made a mistake because I've turned up looking the worse for wear. If I don't get the job I'm finished for sure, I really do need his help.

That was a long night and it must still be early, thought Tom, it's pitch black, I hate the dark mornings. The fog should have lifted by the time I head out to see Stephen, I've got plenty of time to tidy myself up and get a sandwich and a hot cup of coffee, the Late and Early will be open by the time I get there. This is going to be a good day I can feel it in my bones, though that's more likely to be a touch of arthritis, the frost last night was wicked. Wow, two euro just balanced on the kerb this really is my lucky day, it's an omen, I'll keep it for luck it will be a reminder for me in the future. It can represent the day I began to live again, I'll keep it with me always that is if I don't get desperate and need it for food, no I won't have any negative thoughts, not today. Right, I'm warmed up a bit after the coffee and sandwich, they went down a treat and I'm ready to head over to see Stephen. If I've got the job I'll be celebrating tonight, I might even spoil myself and get a cup of coffee to go with my dinner of another sandwich or maybe a roll. I'm getting ahead of myself as usual, God, I don't know what I'll do if Stephen's not around, there I go again bloody negative thoughts I have to think positively. Positive thinking, that can make things happen, no more thinking the worst it may never happen. Almost there now and I think I can see Stephen's van up ahead, yes it's his van alright, this positive thinking is working already. Right Tom, don't blow it, be casual but not too casual, and don't ask him straight away about the job.

'Good morning Stephen, and what a beautiful morning it is.'

'Hello Tom, I didn't see you there, you're out bright and early, did you get sorted last night?'

'I did, Stephen, I got the last available bed and was I glad of it.' A little lie didn't seem very important. 'There was a heavy ground frost and fog this morning, I was afraid I'd get lost and not find my way here.'

'Aye there was a nice bit of frost but the fog has at last lifted and I think we're in for a good day today Tom.'

Tom wondered how long it would take Stephen to get around to telling him if had got the job or not, and he wondered if he was enjoying playing the big boss thing. Tom had no alternative, he had to bide his time until Stephen was ready to put him out of his misery. Finally, after ten minutes of making small talk, Stephen gave Tom the answer he was hoping for.

'I had a word with the little woman last night, and we agreed you could start on a trial basis starting tomorrow, how does that sound Tom?'

'Thanks a million Stephen, and please tell your wife that I really appreciate this. I promise you, you won't regret it, I won't let you down,' said Tom, who was almost in tears.

'You had better not, Tom, you don't know what my wife's like if someone lets her down or crosses her, I'll say no more.'

'What time do you want me to start at tomorrow?' asked Tom excitedly.

'Be here at seven-thirty sharp, I like to get started as early as possible, as the days are short enough at this time of the year.'

'No problem, I'll be here on the dot of seven thirty a.m., goodbye Stephen and thanks again.' Tom was over the moon and he now felt that his life had some purpose. Lately he had been feeling very dispirited and thoughts of ending it all had crossed his mind once or twice, he never used to get depressed, and these feelings were alien to him.

Tom knew there were a few things he had to sort out for the morning, namely finding his P45, which Stephen had warned him to bring with him, or organise to have, as soon as possible. Tom realised that Stephen had been speaking to him and he hadn't heard a word, he was miles away,

'I'm sorry, what was that you were saying?'

'Well I hope this isn't a sign of things to come Tom, I said you'd be doing the trivial jobs to begin with, the fetching and carrying, the cleaning up, oh and of course the tea making'.

'That's fine; I'll do whatever you tell me to do. There is one thing you haven't mentioned Stephen and I hate to bring it up now but how much will I be paid?' asked Tom, wishing that Stephen had mentioned it to start with. Stephen had been waiting for this and a little smile played at the corner of his mouth.

'I won't beat about the bush,' said Stephen, 'six euro per hour to start with and if things work out, well we can talk about that when the time comes. How does that sound to you Tom?'

'Fine,' replied Tom as he tried to hide his disappointment. He was sure that this amount was under the minimum wage and he would make sure to find out his full entitlements as soon as possible. For now, Tom would have to accept Stephen's paltry offer, he knew that as soon as he was on his feet again he would find a better paying job. Stephen gave Tom a pair of overalls they were a size too small but he took them without uttering a word of complaint, he couldn't afford to be fussy before he'd even started work.

'See you 7.30 tomorrow morning and don't be late or I'll have to dock your wages and that wouldn't be a good start now, would it?'

Tom wasn't going to rise to the bait so he smiled as he answered.

'No problem Stephen, no problem.' Tom hoped that his new boss wasn't taking the piss, he wasn't going to let this little power play of Stephen's get to him, he had met many 'Stephens' in his time. These sort of people always had an inflated sense of self-importance and they were usually insecure, and petty minded, Tom let it pass, though he did wonder why Stephen was treating him like this. They had known each other for a few months now and this was the first time that Stephen hadn't treated him as an equal. Tom headed back to the hostel in good time that night, he needed a good night's sleep in readiness for work in the morning. That night, Tom tried to work out what he would actually take home in pay, he would pay little or no tax, but that still wouldn't leave him with much to live on. It was going to be awhile before he'd be able to get a bed-sitter at this rate, there I go again, he thought, letting negative thoughts in. Banish them, that's what he'd do think only good thoughts after all it had been a good day, he'd enjoyed his dinner albeit just a ham and cheese sandwich and a strong cup of coffee, he'd treated himself to celebrate joining the ranks of the employed. Tomorrow would be a new start for him and this time he would get it right, he was being given a chance to turn his life around, he wasn't going to do anything to jeopardise that.

For the next three months Tom worked hard and didn't complain about the wages or the jobs he was expected to do, he took whatever Stephen threw at him, he was determined to prove himself. He was never late for work and he was often the last to leave in the evening, he was a model employee. Stephen eventually had to concede that Tom was a very good worker and he started to show him some respect. Tom was an asset to the business and gradually Stephen came to rely on him more and more, he had to admit that he'd done the right thing giving him a job. Even Stephen's customers took to Tom and quite often they recommended Stephen's company to their friends because of him; he was a good influence on the two lads that he worked with too, and Stephen wondered how he had managed before he'd taken him on. Tom was given more and more responsibility, which he was happy to take on; this showed Stephens trust in him, he proved to be a natural in the paint and decorating business. Tom had a flair for interior design and often customers asked for his opinions with regards to colour schemes and soft furnishings or accessories, Tom had found his niche.

At the end of February, Tom saw an advertisement in the Evening Standard, it was for a handyman to do light maintenance work in exchange for his board and lodging, the ad said that someone who might be able to do some gardening would be an advantage but was not essential. Tom replied straight away and the young widow who had placed the ad was very taken with him and he was offered the room there and then.

Molly Hunt, the young woman looking for help around the house didn't even ask him for references. This was the start of another episode in his life and as expected, Tom was an exemplary lodger and great company for Molly. As usual Stephen ribbed him over his developing relationship with his landlady, not that Tom ever gave him much information about his private life, Stephen just seemed to have a knack or intuition about some things or sometimes he jumped to conclusions.

Molly was a pretty thirty-eight year old and at 5'4" tall she gave the impression of being vulnerable, which wasn't in fact the truth, she was very capable of looking after herself. Molly's husband had died as a result of a brain haemorrhage, a year ago, and unfortunately they didn't have any children, Molly didn't see the likelihood of this happening now. She truly believed that she wasn't meant to have kids why else wouldn't it have happened? This didn't get her down though, she was easy going and she was grateful for what she did have, her family, good friends and a good lodger who subsequently became her lover and her best friend, Molly considered herself lucky. Things were really looking up for Tom and he settled into this new life with the satisfaction of knowing that he had turned a corner and he was happy with the way things were turning out. He turned up for work each day ready for any new experiences that came his way, and continued to learn everything he could about the trade, he was also becoming indispensable to Stephen who relied on him more and more. Stephen gave Tom a spare set of keys for the van and admitted to himself that business had never been better which was mostly down to Tom and the effort he put in. Stephen was on the lookout to buy a second van. By the middle of March, Tom was collecting the two lads he worked with and driving them to whatever jobs they were working on, he also kept an eye on them as requested by Stephen. They were good lads and they worked better under Tom's supervision than they had for Stephen, they didn't resent or question Tom's position or authority, he brought out the best in them. Stephen knew that he had got the best end of the deal; he was now free to do more surveys and more of the unenviable mountain of paperwork. He even got Tom's input about certain work practices; he made use of him and although he sometimes still took advantage of Tom's generous nature, he had given him a generous wage increase; he didn't want Tom looking elsewhere for a job.

Learning the business from the bottom up was Tom's priority and he felt confident that this was progressing at a fast pace, the only fly in the ointment was Stephen's sarcasm towards him and the other lads. There were occasions when Tom had felt like chucking it in but he swallowed his pride and he continued to work and learn all he could from Stephen. Early in April, just before Easter, Tom got a call from Stephen to pick him up from a job he was working on, he was leaving the van on site and he needed a lift home. This would be the first time that Tom got to see where Stephen lived. He was quite looking forward to it, his boss often talked about his home life and family, and Tom felt as if he already knew them personally; they sounded like a lively but nice bunch. On the drive home the two men chatted away, mainly about work and about the next jobs they were going to start on. Stephen often took on too many jobs at one time and he spent a lot of his time travelling between one job and another, trying to keep all his customers happy. Eventually, Tom persuaded Stephen to take on another couple of lads which took the some of the pressure off; he could only do so much; he already worked more hours than anyone else. He remained cheerful and he still carried his lucky coin around with him, which he had found on the 19th October the day he was given this job, a day he would remember for a long time to come. In a way he was paying Stephen back for having given him the break in the first place. They drove out towards Monkstown where Stephen and his family lived since they had got married; Stephen talked incessantly about his wife and about how much she meant to him, he didn't say very much about his children lately. Tom gathered that the children were typical of teenagers everywhere; which meant they were moody, uncommunicative and a drain on his bank balance. Stephen's attitude to his kids had changed in the past couple of months but he hadn't said anything to Tom as to the reason for this. Tom knew better than to ask, he'd been accused in the past of being overly familiar with regards to Stephen's private life; this followed a conversation where Tom voiced a negative opinion against one of Stephen's kids, it was a mistake, which he wouldn't repeat again. A parent is entitled to criticize his offspring but no one else has that right. Tom was well used to his boss ranting and raving, he let him talk away without interruption or comment from himself, Tom knew that this was what was expected of him. Every now and again Stephen gave Tom directions and then fell back into whatever subject he been talking about at the time. Tom only half listened, he nodded or shook his head as required of him; he had other things on his mind. At last Stephen gave him instructions to pull up at a rather grand looking house with a well-landscaped garden on either side of the driveway. Tom was duly impressed, and he thought that this house was very similar to the one in which he had lived a few years ago, but he wasn't envious of his boss. Tom was not expecting an invitation into Stephen's home and he didn't get one, instead he continued to rant and then dismissed Tom with the warning not to be late collecting him in the morning, 7a.m. sharp. There wasn't even a word of thanks or an apology for having delayed Tom from getting home himself; this was so typical of Stephen.

It was late as Tom made his way through the slow moving traffic, back towards the city centre and on to the South Circular road; he made a quick call to Molly to let her know that he was on his way home. Home, the word had a nice ring to it and he smiled in contentment, yes, he thought, he was content. As Tom pulled up at Molly's modest semi detached house in Inchicore, he compared it to Stephen's and instinctively he knew that here was a proper home not just a house. The lights were on in all the downstairs rooms and Tom was looking forward to the reception, which he knew he would get the minute he turned his key in the lock. It was a little after 8p.m. as he opened the front door, he was happy to be home and he looked forward to having dinner with Molly who had held her dinner back in order to eat with him; she treated him like a lord.

Chapter 2

Molly ran to greet Tom as soon as she heard his key turn in the front door, she was genuinely happy to see him. At 5'4" and with curly blond hair and an angelic looking face she always made Tom feel the most important man on the planet; and even though she had had more than her share of hardship and bad luck she always managed to remain cheerful with a ready smile on her face.

Molly truly was one in a million. Tom wondered how he had been so blessed as to meet her just at the right time in his life, kismet, or something like it he thought.

They had hit it off immediately and within two weeks of Tom becoming Molly's lodger he had also become her lover. Tom felt ten feet tall when Molly put her arms around him and hugged him tightly, it was something special and all his cares and worries seemed to melt away; they suited each other and were soul mates.

The smell of beef casserole wafted to the front door and Tom's mouth watered, this was one of his favourite dinners and his shower could wait until he'd eaten. Usually he'd shower first and unwind for half an hour before he could even think about eating anything but he was late tonight and very hungry. Molly had quickly got used to his ways and she planned their meals accordingly, she was a very good cook and a natural homemaker. Just looking at Molly gave Tom shivers down his spine, which was a relatively new experience for him; there was only one other woman, or rather girl, who had this effect on him and that had been years ago. Tom put the thought out of his head and smiled across at Molly, once again he thanked God for his blessings. Molly served up their dinners and they talked as they ate, Tom recounted some of the day's happenings, some funny some not so funny. Tom felt absolutely no pressure when he was with Molly and they could sit in silence or make small talk without either one of them feeling uncomfortable. Molly sat opposite Tom in the small kitchen and she smiled at him in contentment, she never expected to be this happy, not since her husband had died. They finished their dinner and dessert in an amicable silence after which Tom went into the sitting room to catch up on the day's news on the television, he caught the tail end of the news; Gardai in Harcourt Street were looking for witnesses to a crime which had taken place in St Stephen's Green on the 18th October last, following a vicious assault, a young man had died. The young man had been in attacked and the Gardai wanted to hear from anyone who had been in the vicinity or had heard anything that night. Something stirred in Tom's memory but just at that moment Molly, who had finished washing up the dishes came in to join him so he switched off the television set and turned his attention to Molly. Tom was feeling frisky as they headed upstairs to shower and get ready for bed and he put aside any thoughts about the news item he'd heard earlier.

After they'd made love Molly snuggled up to Tom and they talked for a few minutes, Tom told her about taking

Stephen home, Molly had a definite opinion about Stephen even though she hadn't met him she didn't particularly like him. Tom had told her some of the things that he'd had to put up with since going to work for him. Tom wasn't being disloyal to the man who'd given him a break; he was just filling her in on some of his background. She was an expert at reading between the lines, her job as a psychiatric nurse enabled her to do this. In just over ten minutes they were sound asleep; though Tom tossed about during the night, Molly hardly stirred at all.

The alarm clock ringing at 5.30a.m. jolted them both awake and Molly was the first to get up, she went downstairs to get Tom's breakfast; porridge and toast should keep him going for a few hours. She could hear Tom singing in the shower and she smiled to herself, his singing would do the crows out of business. Tom was still singing when he came into the kitchen and sat down to have his breakfast, he was hungry after his exercise last night; he tucked in to the porridge and then finished off the toast and he drank two cups of coffee. Molly had made some sandwiches for Tom to take with him she wasn't in a hurry as she had a day off; she liked doing these small things for him and he appreciated it. By 6a.m. Tom was in the van, having first kissed Molly goodbye, as he drove away from the house he could see Molly in his wing mirror, she would stand there until the van was out of sight; it was her little ritual and Tom was touched by it. Molly wasn't the clingy type, but she said she never wanted to let him out of her sight. Smiling, Tom drove across town and headed over to Stephen's, a quick glance at his watch told him that he was in good time and his boss would have nothing to complain about. It was a beautiful spring morning and the traffic was moving along nicely it didn't take long to get to Stephen's; Tom pulled up at his house at 6.55a.m. No sooner had he switched off the ignition then Stephen was beside the van, his face showed some signs of annoyance and he pulled open the door on the driver's side; he pushed Tom over. Tom moved across to the passenger seat and waited for Stephen to speak. 'That bloody family of mine, why is there always some problem or crisis with them?' said Stephen through gritted teeth. Tom didn't ask what had happened, if Stephen wanted him to know he'd tell him but he didn't enlighten him further. They drove on in silence to where Stephen had left his other van; as he got out he told Tom to get finished up quickly on the job he was doing and get back over to him that afternoon, he needed extra help here. Tom waved and drove off to collect the lads; he knew there wouldn't be a problem getting their job done by the afternoon and by then Stephen would have calmed down. Tom did wonder what it was that had set him off that morning, he guessed that it was probably his kids; it usually was so Tom put it out of his mind. The day flew by, Tom and the lads got back to Stephen at 3p.m. and between them all they got the job done by 4.45p.m.

Stephen was still in a foul mood as they packed up the equipment and loaded up the vans; he told Tom he was going straight home, he had some things to sort out, he said he would call Tom later on to let him know where he was to go to the next day, Tom asked him if he wanted to talk about what was bothering him but he shook his head saying that he'd take care of it; it was a family thing. He drove off without saying another word so Tom packed up the remaining gear and dropped the lads home. Tom understood and wasn't offended. He was glad to be going home early, it had been a long time since he'd finished this early. After dropping the lads off Tom called into the garage; he filled up on diesel for the morning and he bought a bunch of flowers for Molly. His thoughts turned to the coming weekend, he decided to take Molly away to a hotel for a treat; he would book somewhere nice, maybe in Wicklow, and they could relax and enjoy each others company. Tom knew that Stephen wouldn't be too happy, but that was his hard luck. Tom had worked six days a week since he had started working for him and he felt he was entitled to one weekend off, Stephen would probably make a big song and dance about it but that wouldn't bother Tom, he could cope with that. He wouldn't say anything to Molly until he'd it organised, he didn't want to let her down or spoil the surprise.

Tom was right about Stephen's reaction to his looking for the Saturday off he said they had too much work on and he'd need Tom to supervise some of the work. Tom knew that one day off wasn't going to hurt the business; the work schedule could be rearranged to suit Stephen and the lads. If Stephen didn't like it then he'd have to lump it, Tom was going to have the weekend off and that was that. Stephen growled a begrudging O.K., and Tom was pleased that he didn't have to change his arrangements; he knew he deserved the time off and he'd make up the time next week.

As it was Thursday, the lads would be heading off to the pub to spend some of their wages; they never overdid it as they knew they had work the next day. On the odd occasion, Tom went with them, they had a laugh and they enjoyed each others company; they'd have a few beers and play a couple of games of darts and then head away at a reasonable hour. Since Tom and Molly had got together there hadn't been any nights out with the lads and they gave him some stick over it, they weren't serious, they were happy that Tom had someone in his life. The lads got on well with him and he treated them with respect and they repaid him by working hard in return.

That night, Tom told Molly about his plans for the weekend and she was so excited that she danced around the sitting room; she was like a child. Tom was glad that he had stood his ground with Stephen.

Friday dawned with a touch of frost but with clear blue skies and the promise of another sunny day in store, Tom told Molly that he would be home by 4.30p.m. in order that they could get away at a reasonable time. Molly expected to get home at around the same time, they were both looking forward to getting out of Dublin for the weekend; they both headed off to work at the same time. Molly drove a Fiat Punto car, while Tom drove off in the van. The day progressed quite slowly, anything that could go wrong did go wrong; the house they were to work on needed a lot more work doing on it than Stephen had allowed for. The colour scheme for the master bedroom was a hideous avocado colour and the contrast was a vile puce colour; Tom, never ceased to be amazed at some of the colours that people chose, he was sure that some of them were colour-blind, if not maybe they were just blind.

The owners' of the property had their own ideas about what looked good and what didn't and no amount of tactful suggestions could persuade them to change at least one of the colours they had no intention of changing their minds. Tom knew they were making a big mistake, however, it was their choice and they were paying for it, so that was that.

By lunchtime, Stephen had paid them a visit and it was quite clear that his mood hadn't improved on the previous days; Tom thought that it must be fairly serious as it wasn't like Stephen to dwell on things like this. Tom knew that there was nothing he could do as Stephen refused to talk about what was bugging him; he was like a briar and the lads fell in for some unnecessary criticism and verbal abuse. Tom talked to them and diffused the situation which was threatening to escalate out of proportion and he thanked God that it was nearly time for him to pack up for the day, it had been soul destroying. Stephen's tantrums helped no one, Tom had tried to get him to tell him what was bothering him but to no avail, there was nothing else he could do or say so he decided to leave him to it. Some people couldn't be helped they liked the bit of drama in their lives and some people were never happy unless they were complaining; this was another favourite saying of Tom's father, it had a ring of truth to it. Stephen did however manage to tell Tom to have a good weekend; this came as a surprise to Tom who had half expected another lecture about taking the time off. Tom got the van packed up in double quick time and Stephen told him that he would drop the lads home himself; Tom was able to go straight home. This was a first for Stephen and Tom felt slightly guilty that he hadn't tried harder to find out what was wrong with Stephen. The guilty feeling didn't last long and soon Tom was smiling again.

As he pulled up at Molly's, he could see that her car was already there in front of the house, he felt a bit childish at being so excited about going away with Molly, he was going to do everything he could to make this a memorable weekend. Molly had already packed for them both, she couldn't wait to get going; she hurried Tom upstairs to have a quick shower and change out of his work clothes. She had left his good clothes laid out on the bed and she was ready to pack their stuff in the car, Molly wanted this to be a really romantic few days, she wanted to show Tom how she felt about him. It was funny how different people brought out different things in others; she was always shy with her husband and embarrassed about anything sexual in their relationship, she was the opposite when she was with Tom. She had no inhibitions and was quite content to take the lead and initiate the first move in the sex department; or be led as the situation occurred. Her life was so totally different with Tom, not that she had been unhappy with her husband; she just hadn't been that at ease with him. With Tom she could be herself; she was relaxed and at ease with him, which she preferred. This was going to be a lovely break for them, Molly was ready to tell Tom that she had fallen in love with him; she hoped he felt the same way about her.

Tom had finished showering, he hadn't sung in the shower this time, he had a few things on his mind. He was concerned about Stephen, things needed to improve by Monday or working with him would be hell. Tom was slightly nervous about taking Molly away, he too wanted things to be perfect, she deserved that; she made him happier than he'd ever been before. Tom knew that he was in love with Molly and he wanted to tell her this, tonight; he hoped it wasn't too soon after the death of her husband to get so serious. It wasn't as if he was going to propose, but he was going to say the LOVE word, he didn't want this to put her off or change their relationship; he couldn't bear that. He went downstairs and Molly had everything organised so that they could make a quick getaway.

Molly appeared to be a little nervous and Tom wondered if his forth-coming declaration might be too much too soon; maybe she had sensed that Tom was getting serious and she might not be too happy with that. They got into the car, and for the first time in their relationship they were slightly on edge with each other. Tom started up the car and they headed off to the Wicklow hills, and what they both hoped would be an enjoyable time.

Stephen had grudgingly agreed to let Tom take Saturday off. He knew that Tom deserved the break but at the moment he had a lot on his mind; he could have done with having Tom here this weekend. Tom had worked like a Trojan since starting to work for him months ago; this would be his first weekend off in all that time. Stephen had never regretted giving him a job; he had more than been repaid for trusting Tom. If the truth was known, Maura wouldn't have taken him on at all, it was Stephen who had decided to. At present Maura was very distracted with family problems.

Maura was a strong woman both mentally and physically; she was the brains and the driving force behind the business, she also controlled the purse strings. So if Maura hadn't wanted Stephen to give Tom a job, for whatever reason, Tom wouldn't get a job. It wasn't as if she'd actually met him, but from what her husband had told her she didn't need a homeless bum in the company, she didn't want any more trouble than she had already.

Almost from the day she'd married Stephen she realised she'd made a mistake. The fact that she had miscarried so soon after the wedding only served to enforce this opinion; this was what Maura called the conspiracy of life, the world was out to get her, and get her it quite often did. Getting married had all been down to her parents who had put so much pressure on them that they felt they had no choice but to go along with it. Illegitimacy was still an enormous stigma for which the child would suffer for the rest of its life, or so Maura's mother reckoned. Maura had been too young and immature to disagree with her parents, who were used to getting their own way. They were devout Catholics, so divorce was out of the question. Maura, unbeknown to them had contacted a Bishop regarding the possibility of getting an annulment; but she was told in no uncertain terms that this wasn't going to happen. Grow up, and accept your mistakes, she was told. He advised her to work hard at her marriage and start to show some respect for her hard-working husband. He gave her a sermon on the sanctity of marriage and reminded her of the mortal sin she had committed by indulging in fornication. Maura went away feeling like she had got pregnant by herself; the Bishop had told her she was a wicked temptress who should accept her lot and be grateful to her husband for having the decency to marry her in the first place. Maura had had only one previous sexual partner before Stephen; she kept this fact to herself. She became wistful whenever she thought of him, Tomas, where was he and what was he doing now? Their break-up had a devastating effect on Maura. Tomas had got the opportunity of an apprenticeship with a construction company in Germany; he had to take it, it was a chance for him to make something of himself. Maura was too young to go with him; besides the fact that he wouldn't have been able to support her, her family would never have let her go with him. They did like him; but their daughter, they felt, could do much better than him. Maura took up with Stephen as an act of defiance against her parents.

After the miscarriage Maura insisted that they go out more, so they socialised quite a bit during the early years of marriage; Stephen had been attractive in a cuddly sort of way. They tried to make the best of a bad lot, so when Maura fell pregnant and gave birth to their son, Sean, their marriage had settled into a pattern of relative respect for each other.

Maura's parents doted on Sean and they took over; they had set Stephen up with the painting business, but they gave their daughter the controlling interest in it. Stephen was happy enough with this arrangement, he was just glad to be his own boss. In fairness, he worked hard in the early years and the business did well. However after a few years he began to let things slide, not only the business but also his appearance suffered too. Stephen still worked enough to keep the business ticking over, but he lost interest in making a real go of it; he put bread on the table and clothes on their backs but anything else they had was down to Maura and her parents. His in-laws had given their daughter a handsome cheque on her twenty-first, and they continued to give her a very generous monthly allowance; they also set up trust funds for their grandchildren as they came along. Maura looked after her money and she had a tidy sum put by for the future just in case it was needed. By the time Maura had her second child, a girl, her marriage was in name only. Sleeping with her husband had ceased the minute she had found out that she was pregnant with Sarah. Their sex life had been virtually nonexistent for the previous five years anyway. Stephen didn't seem too bothered; as long as he had plenty to eat and enough Guinness to drink he was content with his life. At night he sat in front of the television, drinking cans of Guinness and eating snacks; on the odd occasion that he did the paperwork he made sure he finished in time to nip down to the pub, for a couple of pints. On returning, he'd pig out on the sofa before going up to bed; by which time Maura would be asleep and there would be no need for any conversation.

Shortly after the birth of their daughter, Maura moved into one of the other bedrooms; this truly signalled the end of any sexual contact between them. Maura didn't actually lock her bedroom door, that wasn't necessary; Stephen knew his place, and he had been firmly put in it. His acceptance of this made it easier for Maura to justify her affairs. Their lives continued much the same as before; they were civil to each other, and the children knew no different they wanted for nothing.

Stephen's parents had seldom visited and they would have never remarked about Stephen not sleeping with his wife. His parents had both passed away at an early age. His mother had heart problems for a few years before she died, his father died two years later from stomach cancer; he'd been a heavy smoker and drinker all his life. Stephen was heartbroken after his mother died, he adored her; though she never showed him any real affection, there was still that mother-son bond between them. His father had been abusive towards his mother especially when he'd roll home drunk every weekend; he had tried to protect his mother, but he wasn't strong enough. At least Stephen didn't take after him; he was never violent towards Maura, who had made it eminently clear that he'd be out on his arse if he ever raised his hand to her or their children

Stephen loved his family even if he didn't know how to show it. He had become stuck in his ways even as regards the clothes he wore which were outdated; and according to his children they were hickey looking. Maura had updated his wardrobe on several occasions; once or twice the new clothes would get an airing but then they wouldn't see the light of day again. He really was set in his ways. When Maura felt that the children were old enough to be left in his care; she started to go out with some of her girlfriends on a Friday night, this became a regular outing for her and she loved the time apart. The girls would meet up in town, have a few drinks and then go on to a club afterwards; they didn't always go home together, sometimes they would have male company with them.

Over the years, Maura had several lovers; most of these were casual relationships, one or two were more long term affairs; these ended when Maura felt they were getting too serious, she wasn't prepared to give too much of herself to these men. They met her sexual needs and that was important to her, being young and having a normal sexual appetite, which was never going to be satisfied by her husband. Maura didn't think her children knew about her affairs; as it happened they did, but as they knew no different, this wasn't a problem for them. They thought that this was how all married couples behaved, and their father didn't complain so why should they? Stephen was just happy that Maura wasn't bringing them back to their home or openly flaunting them in his face; he was quite lazy in the sex department, so after fathering the two children, his duty was done. It never crossed his mind that maybe the children weren't his; as it happened they were. They were conceived on the rare occasions when Maura had taken a drop too much whiskey; she'd fallen into bed with him, but remembered nothing the next day. Apart from a feeling of revulsion, Maura promised herself that it wouldn't happen ever again. Maura kept that promise.

Maura's parents moved out of Dublin when Sean was six and Sarah was just a year old; they had bought a cottage in Tramore, Co. Waterford. This had been a holiday destination that they'd fallen in love with over the years. It had been a big wrench moving away from their daughter and grandchildren, but they would still see a lot of them when they'd come to visit, which they hoped would be often. Maura was particularly down about the move, but after the first few visits to her parents she realised that it had an upside to it; Maura now had more time to herself. Her children spent long weekends and holidays in the seaside resort, they had the best of both worlds; even Stephen was more relaxed when they were away. He was inclined to think that his son was more intelligent than him, Maura would agree with him. They could do no wrong in her eyes and this never changed over the years, this caused some tension down the years between her and her husband. As usual Stephen acquiesced to keep the peace; he believed that it was a woman's job to rear the children and take care of the house.

Shortly after Sean was born Maura hired a cleaning lady, who came three times a week; this left Maura free to indulge her son more than she already did. When Sarah came along the cleaning lady came in full time, five days a week, Maura was very happy with this arrangement; she paid her well and in return she didn't have a tap of housework to do. From the laundry to the cooking and even the occasional babysitting her cleaner, Jean was indispensable and totally trustworthy; she was loyal to Maura who appreciated her and rewarded her for this. The Breslin household ran smoothly for the most part.

Stephen took himself off to work each morning and when he came home in the evening he regaled his family with various stories of his day, he seldom thought to ask Maura about her day. She listened to how Stephen had blown his top at a young lad who was working for him; the poor lad hadn't cleaned the paintbrushes properly and two of them had gone hard. The way Stephen went on it was almost a hanging offence; Maura switched off when he was having a rant, she had become very adept at doing this. She was able to plan her nights out while at the same time half listen to his ranting; he didn't even notice that she wasn't answering or even taking any part in the conversation. Maura did actually hear what she needed to hear and then filtered out the rest. This was how their marriage continued throughout the years that they were together; they were indifferent to each other, they led separate lives, though Stephen never admitted it outside his home. He plodded along pretending everything was fine and he even boasted about how much his wife loved him. Maura knew about this but she didn't mind, there was no harm in him dreaming.

One of Maura's one-night stands was an employee of Stephen's; he was three years younger than her and he professed to being in love with her, when Stephen found out he was absolutely gutted. It taught Maura a valuable lesson; she would never do the dirty on her own doorstep. Stephen sacked the lad straight away; he didn't give him any notice or reference, and the lad had the sense not to ask for any. Maura contacted the lad behind Stephen's back, she gave him a glowing reference and a month's wages; she felt she was to blame for the lad getting the push.

Maura wondered why Stephen didn't have any affairs. He wasn't that undesirable; she guessed that he was too lazy to bother. Most of the time she was too busy with her own life to care what was going on in Stephen's, she did keep an eye on the business without him ever realising she was doing it. Over the years Stephen realised it was better not to rock the boat and just go along with Maura and what her family wanted; his life was going along nicely thank you very much, he had no worries to speak of.

When Stephen's mother died, his father was absolutely devastated; he suddenly realised what a mess he'd made of his life, he knew he'd been a complete bastard to her and their son, he was genuinely sorry. Stephen asked Maura if his father could stay with them for a while, until he had come to terms with her death. Of course Maura agreed, she wasn't happy but she had one condition that was that he didn't drink as long as he was under their roof. Bob agreed. A month after his wife's death, Bob started to complain of heartburn and pain in his stomach; Maura thought it was probably withdrawal symptoms as he had kept his word and not had a drink during that time. Stephen gave him some antacid and muttered something about it serving him right for his past sins; he was in a world of his own, he thought he was the only one grieving. Maura was glad when he went back to work, she couldn't bear to have the two of them under her feet. While they spent time together during the day, Maura learnt a lot of things about Stephen's childhood more than he'd ever told her. What she learned actually shed some light on the way Stephen behaved with her; it was too late to change things but it showed him in a different light. He had grown up with an alcoholic father who was physically abusive towards his mother, but had never raised his voice or his hand to his son.

As a child Stephen had loathed confrontation, this continued into his adult life. His favourite saying was, go with the flow. He had often tried to protect his mother from the abuse but he wasn't strong enough; he grew up hating his father for making him feel so weak and inadequate. He was still a bit afraid of his father, he wouldn't turn his back on him but he wasn't going to pander to his every wish.

Chapter 3

Bob was just sixty-two years old when his wife died. He finally admitted to himself that his alcoholism had ruined any chance of being close to his son. For the past few years his alcohol consumption had been negligible, due mainly to having a gastric ulcer, which took a long time to heal. Living in his son's home and not drinking any alcohol didn't cause him any problems; in some ways he was glad that he had been forced to stop drinking, it would probably save his life.

Bob didn't expect his son to ever forgive him for the way he had treated his mother, and he didn't deserve forgiveness. He was grateful to have been taken into his son's home; he liked being part of a family again. It didn't take Bob long to realise that his son's marriage was in trouble; he knew about the sleeping arrangements and he blamed himself in part for not being a better role model. At least Stephen wasn't following in his footsteps; he wasn't abusive or a drunk which was a blessing and a little consolation to Bob. Bob liked his grandchildren, though they were a bit spoilt and he could see that they were used to getting everything they wanted; he could foresee problems in the future if they weren't taken in hand soon. He kept these thoughts to himself, Maura had a sharp tongue and she wouldn't welcome his opinion on the way the children were being raised.

When Stephen went back to work, after his mother's funeral, Bob and Maura spent quite a bit of time talking about the past. This gave Maura an insight in to what made her husband the way he was. Bob had never been unfaithful to his wife; this was probably because he was always too drunk to perform. Stephen was addicted to junk food; his father was addicted to alcohol. Maura began to realise that Bob's digestive trouble might not be due to withdrawal symptoms, it might be something else altogether. He genuinely seemed to be in quite a lot of pain; Maura had heard him vomiting a few times over the weekend, his clothes had started to look too big on him, which she should have picked up on sooner. A visit to the doctor was now a necessity. Maura arranged for Bob to see her doctor who immediately booked him in for a Barium Meal, two days later. Stephen refused to take the day off to bring his father to the clinic for his X-ray; Maura did the needful instead.

Bob was unable to keep the Barium down; he threw up all over himself and the attending nurse, the radiographer contacted the consultant gastric surgeon; a gastroscopy was ordered for the same afternoon. When Maura had brought her father-in-law to the clinic he had asked her to stay with him; he was afraid of what might be found. The phone rang in reception and Maura was called up to the desk; she was then asked to go to the Day Ward where Bob had been taken, Maura had a bad feeling about this. On arriving in the Day Ward, Maura overheard two nurses discussing the man who was to have a gastroscopy that afternoon; the signs weren't looking good for this poor man, they said.

Instinctively Maura knew that it was Bob they were talking about and she wasn't pleased that they were talking so openly about him; they weren't to know who she was. She stood listening to them until they sensed that she was probably a relation of the man they were discussing; they both went scarlet when Maura gave her name and requested to be taken to see her father-in-law. When she entered his room she was shocked by his appearance. In the two hours since she'd last seen him he had aged at least ten years; he was as white as a sheet and he seemed to have shrunk in size. Even his voice had shrunk. Maura tried not to let him see how shocked she was, for his sake she kept her voice light and cheerful.

Bob wasn't fooled by her light heartedness; he'd seen the looks exchanged between the medical staff, he knew that there was something seriously wrong and that could mean cancer. They made small talk until the orderly came in to take Bob off to have the test; just as he was wheeled out Maura's mobile rang, she had forgotten to switch it off earlier she knew instinctively that it was Stephen so she switched it off. Maura wasn't ready to talk to Stephen, she wanted to wait till the procedure had been done, and the results mightn't be as bad as they feared. The time passed very slowly until Bob was brought back to his room; as expected he looked ghastly, he was very drowsy but he was able to tell Maura that she shouldn't have waited. Maura reminded him that he'd asked her to stay and besides she had nothing else planned for the day. He slept for about half an hour and woke just as the Consultant entered the room. Mr Gerraghty introduced himself; Maura gave him the once over. He was a tall man in his late forties or early fifties and very attractive looking; distinguished is a word that came to her mind. Bob was fully alert now and anxious to get the results, be they good or bad. Mr Gerraghty didn't beat about the bush when he told Bob that he had a large growth, tumour to be more precise, in his stomach. A biopsy had been taken during the gastroscopy and he'd have the results first thing in the morning. Regardless of the result of the biopsy the tumour had to be removed as soon as possible; the next morning would be a good time for the surgery to be performed. Mr Gerraghty didn't give him an option; this was what was going to happen, Bob wouldn't be going home this afternoon.

There were several procedures to be carried out that afternoon; blood tests, chest X-ray and an examination by the anaesthetist were arranged. Bob didn't put up any objections, he needed time to get his head around it; everything was happening so fast. Maura couldn't find the right words to say to him so she made up an excuse that she needed to collect some dry cleaning from a place in town. She told her father-in-law that she'd be back that evening with Stephen. Bob didn't want Stephen told all the facts but Maura insisted that he had a right to be told the truth and Maura was not one to be argued with; Bob thought his son would feel that he was getting his just desserts for his past treatment of his wife.

When Maura left the clinic she headed straight to the café across the road. After ordering a coffee she thought of how to tell Stephen what was happening with his father. She ordered a second coffee before switching her mobile back on, Stephen hadn't left a message so she keyed in his number and took a deep breath as she waited for him to answer. Maura gave her husband the bare facts as she understood them and waited for his reaction. The call lasted a mere three minutes; Stephen was busy and he said he'd see her at home at the usual time, he even asked what they were having for dinner before hanging up. Maura wasn't expecting him to break down but she certainly hadn't expected this reaction, or rather lack of it. She herself was on the verge of tears, which surprised her; she wasn't given to such emotions, Stephen had to be in shock, it would take time to sink in. Maura expected Stephen to call her back in a few minutes when he'd realised what she'd told him.

He didn't.

Maura headed home, she wanted to get a few things together for Bob. He'd need some toiletries and pyjamas; she'd bring him in the book he'd been reading, a thriller by Harlan Coben; she hoped it would take his mind off the surgery he would be having the next day. Maura gave Jean a brief outline of what had transpired that day; she asked if she could come back at 7p.m. so they could go in to see Bob that night. Jean was very obliging and it would be no problem for her to come back to baby-sit the children.

At 6 o'clock Stephen arrived home from work and started the conversation by giving out about the traffic, he was ignoring the most important part, his father. Maura quickly silenced him, she told him to pull himself together; today was not about him, it was about his father. For the first time in their marriage Stephen raised his voice to his wife. He had understood exactly how serious the situation with his father was, he just couldn't feel much sympathy towards him; his father didn't deserve it. As far as Stephen was concerned his father's cancer was a form of punishment, meted out by God for the years of abuse he had dealt out to his wife. Maura was gobsmacked, her husband had never spoken so harshly in all the time she'd known him; this was so out of character that she was sure she had misheard him. Once Stephen got started it was hard for him to stop, the years of suffering in silence burst out in such a torrent that he was actually frothing at the mouth. Maura feared that he'd have a heart attack if he didn't calm down soon. Putting her hand on his arm, Maura gently led him to the armchair and sat him down; he let himself be led by her. He had physically exhausted himself and was now ashamed of his outburst; he burst into tears. Maura wasn't sure what to do or how to handle the situation so she did nothing. It was probably best if Stephen could let his emotions out, that way he wouldn't fall apart when he went to see his father. The dinner was almost ready to be served up so Maura called the children to come down and talk to their father; Stephen was not going to tell the children that their grandfather was in hospital, he was going to tell them that he was going to stay with a friend; he was going to keep it brief so as not to frighten them.

The dinner was eaten in relative silence, Maura noticed that Stephen's appetite had diminished, she didn't know if this meant anything or not. After loading the dishwasher Maura went upstairs to get ready to go back to see Bob, she could hear her husband talking to someone on the phone, he then went to his room, he showered and was changed in twenty minutes. Downstairs Maura opened the door to Jean, who, as usual was right on time; Jean asked Stephen to give her regards to Bob and to wish him well for tomorrow. Stephen was touched by her concern. When they reached the clinic, Maura led the way through the maze of corridors to Bob's room, he was sitting up in bed watching television and his colour was much better than it had been earlier in the day. The three of them made small talk for about ten minutes while Maura unpacked the bag she'd brought in, arranging things neatly in the locker. Maura told the two men that she needed a cup of coffee and she headed out to give them some time together on their own. It was a relief to get out of the room; Maura wasn't very good with sick people, though she had coped very well earlier in the day, it was down to Stephen now. The coffee shop was busy but the service was good, Maura found an empty seat away from the door. She was a people watcher and this was as good a place to watch people as anywhere; however she couldn't stay here all night, she had to go back to the two men.

It was obvious that they'd both been crying Maura was relieved that they had stopped before she'd come back; she wasn't hard, she just didn't like to see grown men cry. It was a sign of weakness and Maura didn't like weak men.

They had lingered over their goodbyes, neither wanting to be the first to go. Maura took the lead and stood up and Stephen followed suit, they then took their leave of Bob, who smiled and told them not to visit him the next night. Bob knew he'd be groggy from the anaesthetic and he knew he'd have the results of the biopsies; he would prefer to be on his own when he got these, he needed time alone to take it all in. Stephen and Maura agreed, but they both knew that they'd be there first thing in the morning and they would be there when he came round after theatre; this wasn't the time for Bob to be on his own.

Maura thought that it was a miracle that Stephen had managed to put his dislike of his father aside; he'd really shown his forgiving nature, which Maura already knew existed. They drove home in silence, each lost in their own thoughts. Maura was thinking that another death so soon after his mother's would have a devastating effect on her husband. Stephen was thinking that his father was a strong man; he'd get through this and become strong again, the thought never entered his head that his father wouldn't recover.

When they arrived home they found that Jean had put the children to bed, after first bathing them and then reading them their favourite stories; Maura was delighted she couldn't face their questions right now. Apart from being tired Maura wanted to wind down and relax after the day she'd had but she offered to drive Jean home. Stephen stepped in and said he'd take Jean home; Maura had done more than her fair share that day, he had to be strong now. Maura took a quick shower, and then went downstairs to pour herself a large brandy; she added a couple of ice cubes and settled herself on the sofa. Within minutes she was fast asleep without having touched her brandy; that was how Stephen found her on his return. For a few minutes he just stared down at his wife; he suddenly realised how much he needed her and depended on her, tears filled his eyes he was overwhelmed with affection for her. Stephen wanted to take her in his arms but he was afraid of rejection, he couldn't deal with that, not tonight. Gently he touched her shoulder and immediately Maura was wide awake and for a moment she wondered what Stephen was doing; he had a strange expression on his face. Maura remembered the events of the day and she offered to pour a drink for Stephen, he was probably in need of one.

For the first time in years they had a real conversation, not that it would change anything in their relationship; too much had gone on for that to happen. They talked for over an hour, discussing what might or might not be the outcome of Bob's operation and biopsy. It was agreed that he would stay with them for the foreseeable future. If he required a nurse then they'd arrange it, he would want for nothing. In the morning Maura and Stephen fielded questions from their children about the whereabouts of their grandfather; Maura didn't want to say too much until she knew all the facts about Bob's condition, she fobbed them off with some story about Bob going to visit an old friend, they accepted this explanation. Sean was only eight years old, Sarah was three; both were too young to be told the possible seriousness of their grandfather's illness. Sean was very sensitive for his age; he'd taken his grandmother's death badly, even though he wasn't particularly close to her. When Maura's parents moved to Co. Waterford, two years ago, Sean had become very withdrawn and difficult to deal with. It took a long time to get through to him and convince him that he would still see a lot of them; Maura didn't want the same problems this time. Stephen hadn't had to deal with Sean's tantrums and his bedwetting; he left Maura to cope with what he called women's work.

Jean arrived early, which was a blessing as Maura had had enough of answering Sean's questions; she didn't like lying to her children. Maura had a quick word with Jean regarding what she'd told her son about where Bob was; Maura could rely on her not to say anything about where he really was. They would talk to their children when they knew the full extent of his illness, until then they needn't be burdened unnecessarily.

When Stephen and Maura got to the clinic Bob was already in surgery so they went to the nurses' station and spoke to the ward sister. They were told that Bob could be in surgery for 3 or 4 hours and then in recovery before being brought back to his room, later that day. If all went well Bob would be back in his room by mid-afternoon; he'd have a nurse with him for the rest of the day and the night as well. Maura and Stephen were advised to go for a coffee or take a walk around the grounds; they would be contacted if there were any news about Bob. It was hard for them to settle in the coffee shop and walking around outside didn't help either; they took turns walking up and down the corridors, but the time dragged by. Finally a nurse told them that Bob was in the recovery ward, his surgery had gone well. The nurse wanted them to get away from the clinic for a few hours; she said that they would be contacted if there were any change in his condition. Maura wished they wouldn't keep saying that, she felt it was tempting fate; however she was glad to get out, though she sensed that Stephen would have preferred to stay.

When they got outside they both switched on their phones; Maura rang home to let Jean know that Bob was out of theatre, she wanted to know if Sean had got off to school on time. Jean had everything under control and she told Maura not to worry about the children, she would stay as long as necessary. Maura relayed this information to Stephen who had been talking to the lads who worked for him; he had told them he'd drop in on them in the morning and for them to carry on with what they were doing. Stephen was just going through the motions right now so Maura didn't interfere; she let him make whatever arrangements he wanted. Neither of them ate much lunch and they were back in the clinic within an hour; they had another hour to wait before Bob was wheeled back to his room.

As expected, Bob was as white as a sheet and attached to a lot of monitors; there were a lot of tubes attached to various parts of his body. Stephen shook; he hadn't been prepared for what his father would look like, and Maura was afraid that he was going to faint. Bob looked old and frail. Maura took control and taking hold of her husband's arm to steady him she guided him to the chair beside his father's bed. A nurse who was checking the monitors said that it was quite normal to be attached to so many tubes after gastric surgery; they shouldn't be alarmed by the beeps and other noises that came from the machines, this was all normal as well. Just as Maura asked when the consultant would be round, he appeared in the doorway; he was dressed in an expensive looking suit, Maura loved men in suits.

Mr Gerraghty read the notes sent down from the recovery ward and seemed satisfied with them he then checked Bob's dressing, again he seemed satisfied; he finally turned his attention to Maura and Stephen who had been watching him with admiration and respect. As Mr Gerraghty was about to speak Bob opened his eyes and gave his son and daughter-in-law a small smile. The consultant asked his patient how he was feeling, before telling him that he was pleased with the surgery he'd performed. He explained that Bob had had a rather large tumour removed, it had been malignant; he was happy with the surgery and he assured Bob that he would soon be feeling a lot better. Mr Gerraghty added that he had performed a temporary colostomy; this would give Bob's internal organs a chance to heal. Bob wasn't really taking any of this in and he drifted off to sleep. Mr Gerraghty said he'd be back to see his patient in the morning; he'd go through this with Bob when he was more alert. Stephen thanked him and shook his hand. Maura was afraid he wouldn't let go. They sat with Bob for another hour and a half during which time he woke several times for a few minutes each time; he didn't complain about anything. The nurse told them that Bob's vital signs were all good and strong; what he needed now was a good night's sleep, so they should go home and try to get some sleep themselves. The nurse would be looking after him that evening until her shift finished at 8p.m.; another nurse would take over for the night shift, she reassured them that Bob would be well cared for. Reluctantly Stephen and Maura left, they knew that that was the sensible thing to do; the dedication of the nursing staff had been obvious even to them.

They were both exhausted when they arrived home and the delicious smell of roast lamb made their mouths water; they hadn't really eaten since breakfast. Jean had made up the bed in the spare room where she sometimes slept over when the need arose; she thought this was one of those times, Maura and Stephen were grateful for her thoughtfulness. It would take the pressure off them in the morning, they wouldn't have to rush around getting the children organised, and Stephen would have time to drop in on the lads as he'd promised. Maura went through to the den where the children were playing with some of their toys; Sean eyed her suspiciously and waited to hear where she'd been. Maura told him that soon, Bob, was going to be moving in permanently with them; and she had been out looking for some new furniture for his room; Stephen had gone with her because he'd know his father's taste better than her. Sean wasn't fully convinced that his mother was telling the truth, but he'd let it go for now; it would be nice having his grandfather around, he hadn't seen that much of him in the past.

Stephen and Maura saw a big change in Bob the next morning, he was sitting up in bed and his colour was much better. He'd had a good night and the nurses had got him out of bed to sit in an armchair while they changed his bed; they shaved him and gave him a bed bath before going off from the night shift. Bob was going to be kept there for about eight to ten days; which would give Maura time to redecorate the room that he'd be staying in, this would convince Sean that she was telling the truth. Bob's recovery progressed rapidly and three days later Stephen felt that he should go back to work, Maura agreed; she'd had enough of his company by now. Maura got into a routine of visiting Bob first thing in the morning for an hour or two, and then she'd go home to supervise the decorating of his room. On one of her visits to see Bob she got talking to Mr Gerraghty, Tony, who she was attracted to and she let him know that she was available for a night out, if he was interested. He was. They arranged to meet up at a small but exclusive restaurant twenty miles from where Maura lived; Tony had his reputation to think of. Their affair continued for two months after Bob had been discharged from the clinic. On one of their visits to a hotel, mid-afternoon, Tony happened to ask after Bob's health, Maura was surprised as he always kept his work separate from his private life. She told him that Bob was in good form and she asked Tony why he was asking.

'I was just wondering if there were any signs that the carcinoma had returned yet; that's why I asked.' Maura was stunned.

'What do you mean, returned? You said you'd got it all when you operated.'

'I'm sorry sweetheart; you must have misunderstood what I said.'

'No. No I didn't misunderstand, you said you were happy with the surgery; what's changed?'

'My dear Maura, I was pleased with my operating skills, and yes I had removed as much of the tumour as possible; but I'm not God, I don't perform miracles. I'm sorry that it wasn't made clear to you at the time, your father-in-law only has about ten to twelve months to live.'

How could they have missed this vital piece of information? Maura was absolutely stunned. What, or how, was she going to tell Stephen? He'd been so much happier since his father had moved in with them; he'd actually forgiven him for his bad treatment of his mother. How would Maura explain how she knew this without Stephen finding out about her affair?

This news showed the wonderful Mr Tony Gerraghty in a different light, Maura would not be seeing him again socially; for some reason she felt he had betrayed her, she knew this wasn't logical but it was how she felt. Tony said she was being melodramatic but it was her choice if she wanted to end the affair; he'd miss her but he could live with her decision. He told her to get Bob to see his own G.P., that way Bob would be told the news without involving Maura or himself. Maura never saw Tony again.

Maura went home that afternoon feeling as sick as a dog, she wasn't going to lie to Bob or Stephen, neither of them deserved that. Stephen would be shocked to hear the news about his father; she wasn't sure how he would react to her affair. She never made any mention to the fact that she been unfaithful before now, Stephen was well aware of this; she wasn't going to rub his nose in it. Both men listened to what she had to say in silence. Bob thought that Mr Gerraghty had abused his position of trust but he was sure that Maura wasn't an innocent party. Stephen only heard the part about his father's prognosis, he was in total shock. Maura didn't matter. Nothing mattered. There would be no recriminations what was done was done.

Chapter 4

It was another seven months before Bob showed any sign that the cancer was back, during which time he had become close to his grandchildren. It had been decided to tell Sean the truth about Bob's condition; Sarah was still too young to understand, so she wasn't told the full story. As expected Sean took the news badly, he became bad tempered and he started stealing money from Maura's purse; no one seemed to know how to deal with him, he was a law unto himself. Maura vowed to sort him out when things settled down; she didn't think he would stay mad for long he was only eight years old.

Bob had been hoping that there had been a mistake when Maura told him about the prognosis from Mr Gerraghty; he couldn't believe that a top consultant like Mr Gerraghty would have risked his career for a few nights with Maura. Yes, he had to admit that she was an attractive woman, but so were millions of others; what was so special about Maura?

Bob had contacted his own doctor, after Maura's revelations; he didn't have any good news to tell him, so that was that. He was dying. It was hard for Bob to accept, he'd had second and third opinions they were all the same; he had secondary cancers and they weren't going to go away, they were inoperable.

Living with his son and his family was the only good thing that had happened to him in the last year, he appreciated all they'd done for him; Stephen even said he'd forgiven him for the past. Bob had wanted to go into a nursing home or hospice when the time came, but Stephen and Maura had vetoed this suggestion; he was going to stay at home with them, it's where he belonged now.

Maura had always been the practical one and she was taking charge, she had already been onto nursing agencies, which provide nurses on a private basis, they weren't cheap but they could afford it, or rather Maura could afford it.

Stephen wasn't running the business, as he should be; he seemed to have lost interest, someone was going to have to talk to him and that meant Maura. Bob, usually an early riser, now stayed in bed till lunchtime; he didn't stay up much after dinner, he hadn't the energy. Stephen still believed that his father was going to get better; he thought that it was good that his father was resting; it would build up his strength. Both Maura and Bob had tried to explain that this wasn't going to happen and Bob didn't have the strength to deal with his son's constant cheeriness. Physically the pain was becoming more severe, but that could be controlled with pain relief; the mental pain wouldn't go away though and Stephen was responsible for a lot of that mental anguish that Bob was suffering.

Maura had been putting off talking to Stephen about his father but she couldn't ignore his behaviour concerning his unwillingness to accept that his father hadn't long to live. That night, after the children had gone to bed Maura insisted that they sit down and talk about Bob's condition. When Maura put her mind to it she could get through to her husband, she knew that it would be better if he accepted things now rather than after his father died; for all their sakes. So far Bob had not required a nurse, Maura and Jean were managing between them, and Bob was a good patient; he could still get out of bed to use the toilet. Jean often helped to shave him if he was feeling weak; she got on really well with him and for his part he didn't resent her helping out. Bob had noticed Sean's change in behaviour and he offered to try to explain the situation to him; Maura declined his offer, if anyone were going to talk to her son it would be her.

Stephen listened to his wife as she went on about his father not having long to live, he knew that what she was saying was true, he just didn't want to admit it; because then it would be there out in the open and Maura would keep mentioning it, and all too quickly it would happen.

Stephen acquiesced; he agreed to have a heart to heart talk with his father the next day. While Maura was getting through to her husband she decided to tackle the problem of the business; one of the lads who had been working for Stephen had packed in the job and the other lad was threatening to do the same. Again Stephen agreed to sort things out; the last thing he wanted was Maura interfering in his work practises. All in all they covered a lot of things that had been put on the long finger, while Bob's illness had taken centre stage.

The next two months passed by much like the previous ones, except that Bob's appetite had diminished to such an extent that he didn't have the strength to get up at all during the day. A commode was installed beside his bed to save his distress at the very odd accident that had occurred, unbeknownst to him. Maura left Jean to deal with these accidents, Jean was more than willing to help out, and she knew Maura didn't have the stomach for such things. The local priest visited Bob on a regular basis and this seemed to bring him some comfort. Three weeks before Bob passed away he was anointed which gave him great peace of mind. He stopped taking any pain relief; saying that he was no longer in any pain; Stephen now realised that his father's death was imminent; and he was barely able to hold it together. Maura felt bad for him and she tried to support him as best she could, Stephen never made things easy for himself and now was no different to any other time.

On the morning of Bob's passing, which was peaceful, Stephen had gone to work at seven thirty; he hadn't looked in on his father who had gone into a coma, he might not have gone to work if he had. It was left up to Maura to call in the doctor and get Stephen home again; Bob didn't wait for his son to come home. Maura had sat with her father-in-law as he took his last breath; she hoped that she would never have to go through anything like that again; she had grown fond of Bob and she knew why he had turned to drink. In the not too distant future, Stephen was going to be told the truth about why his father had been the way he had been; Maura felt he should hear the truth, no matter how hard it would be for him.

On a cold and wet March morning Bob was laid to rest beside his 'long suffering' wife and with his family to see him off.

April started off the way March had ended, wet and windy. The Breslin family remained downbeat after their recent loss; Maura decided that they needed cheering up and a holiday was just what they needed. Never one to procrastinate, she booked them a two-week holiday in Spain from the 10th of April; this would include the Easter holidays. They would still be back in time for Bob's month's mind Mass on the 27th. Maura was pleased that she'd made the booking, though the rest of the family didn't show much enthusiasm, but Maura knew they'd enjoy themselves once they got there. She knew that they could all do with the break and she loved the sun and heat, Stephen preferred the shade.

On the day of departure the whole family appeared happy to be getting away and Jean assured them that she'd look after everything at home for them; she had a lot to do while they were away. Jean was going to do a big spring clean of the house while they were away, not that the house was in any way dirty but Jean thought that the smell of death still lingered in the room where Bob had died.

The weather was brilliant in Torremolinos and there was something to amuse each of the family. In particular, Maura enjoyed being the life and soul of the hotel bar each night she was in her element. Sean and Sarah were sharing the room with their parents and they were up at 7a.m. every morning; regardless of the time they went to bed at night. Stephen let his wife have a lie in, he knew that she'd need the extra hour, so he took the children down to the pool before breakfast; they enjoyed this time together. After their swim they went back to their room to wake Maura up so they could all go down to breakfast together like one happy family. There was only one night that Maura flirted outrageously with one of the other guests who was in his early twenties and single. Stephen could see what was going on and he resigned himself to the fact that his wife would be sleeping elsewhere that night. He had a pleasant surprise when Maura came to bed in her own room he was so pleased that he didn't mention her flirtatious behaviour. Despite Stephen's initial misgiving about the holiday he actually enjoyed it once he was there, Sean and Sarah did as well; the whole family were benefiting from it. All in all, Maura was glad that they were all having a good time. Stephen promised to get motivated and make an effort in the business; he was lucky that Maura hadn't been getting on his back about his lack of interest in his work. Stephen wondered if he should make a pass at his wife and attempt to seduce her, then he thought about it again and decided it was too much of an effort on his part. He knew Maura needed sex and as long as she didn't flaunt her affairs in front of him it was O.K. for her to have casual affairs; he knew that Maura would be careful with regards to picking up infections and sexually contracted diseases. He never gave a thought as to why he wasn't interested in sex so consequently he didn't mention it to his doctor; it was just one of those things and he accepted it. It didn't mean that he didn't love Maura, because he did and he honestly believed that she loved him. Stephen was grateful to Maura for the way she helped with his father during his illness, she could have insisted that he go into a hospice or have a nurse but she didn't. They were all a little sad when the holiday came to an end; it had been a few years since they'd had a family holiday.

They arrived back in Dublin at 6a.m. on the 24th of April and thankfully the weather was mild, a change from when they'd left. Jean had filled the fridge with the essentials so they didn't have to go out shopping that morning. Sean and Sarah checked their rooms to make sure that all their stuff was still there; meanwhile Stephen and Maura ventured into Bob's old room and were pleased to find that there had been changes made to it. Jean had moved the furniture around and added a few little things to make the room more cheerful looking; she had included a vase of daffodils which brightened it up. She had done a great job, which made it easier for them; they didn't keep seeing Bob lying there waiting to die. There was no longer an unpleasant smell and Maura wouldn't have to think about redecorating the room there was no need to now. Both Maura and Stephen made a few phone calls before going to bed to catch up on some sleep; the children had gone earlier, they'd had an early start that morning.

Sean and Sarah were the first to wake and they were starving, it was almost 3p.m.; they hadn't eaten since breakfast. Sarah called her mother who was already in the shower, they let Stephen sleep on for another hour before Sean was sent to get him up; Maura knew he would have trouble sleeping that night if he didn't get up then. Sean had one more day of the Easter holiday left; he was quite looking forward to going back to school, as he missed his mates. Sarah was going to start in nursery school this term; she would be there from 9a.m. to 12p.m., three mornings a week. Maura was going to miss her but she felt that she would benefit from mixing with other children of the same age as herself. This would leave Maura with a lot more spare time on her hands; she would have to find something to fill it with. Stephen jokingly suggested that she could do the books for him and they'd save some money on their accountant's fees; Maura gave him one of her withering looks, which shut him up immediately. Maura did have a good knowledge of book-keeping and she was au fait with general office procedures, but the idea of working 'for' Stephen didn't appeal to her one bit. An idea however, was beginning to formulate in her mind, she'd have to give it some serious thought; but not just now.

Maura had a long conversation with Jean on the phone;

she told her that she needn't have moved back home just because they were back from their holiday, she was welcome to stay as long as she liked. Jean was glad that Maura felt like that, however she was adamant that she liked her own space and her own home; Maura suddenly realised that she had never actually set foot in Jean's house, she had never been invited to. Come to think of it Maura knew very little about her indispensable housekeeper, this was something that she must remedy in the near future. The conversation ended with Maura asking Jean if she'd continue to work the five days a week; she thanked her for the hundredth time for all she'd done while they were away, there would be a nice bonus in with her wages this week. Maura was determined not to lose Jean so she often put a little extra in with her wages. Jean didn't need to work but she did need to feel wanted and she wasn't going to offend Maura by refusing the bonus even though she hadn't actually put in any extra hours while they were away; she also had the use of their home and all its conveniences.

Life was starting to get back to normal in the Breslin household with Stephen going back to work the day after they arrived back from their fortnight in Spain; he advertised for a young lad to learn the painting and decorating trade while earning a reasonable wage while training. Maura offered to interview the applicants but the offer was turned down by Stephen, who wasn't sure if she was joking or not. Maura was feeling in need of some male company so she arranged a girls' night out for the next night, even though it was only Wednesday; her girlfriends had missed her company over the last few months. Maura hadn't liked to go out on the 'pull' while her father-in-law was so sick, even she had a conscience. Stephen was happy enough to look after the children, once they went to bed they stayed there; Maura deserved a night out and all that that entailed.

Maura met up with her friends for a few drinks and they certainly had a lot of catching up to do. Before they headed off to their favourite nightclub they agreed to meet up again on the Friday night to continue catching up on all the gossip and scandal that they had missed over the past months. For a few seconds Maura experienced a feeling of shyness, this was so unlike her that it took her by surprise but she was determined to cast this feeling aside. For the first time since her teenage years Maura felt vulnerable, the last time that she had felt this way was when her parents stopped her from going to Germany with her first love, Tomas. While her parents were in Dublin for Bob's funeral they had talked at length about her teenage years and Maura understood why they had prevented her from going with Tomas; she was too young and immature. Maura didn't resent or blame her parents for how things had turned out and now that she was a parent herself she knew that she'd do exactly the same thing if her daughter were in that position. It was hard to believe that she was in agreement with her parents over how they handled the situation as it happened; she certainly didn't feel that way at the time. Maura had grown up since having her own children and that was what was supposed to happen.

Maura needed a change of direction in her life or otherwise she'd get stuck in a rut, she had a few ideas floating around in her head; she just needed to get her act together and decide in which direction she was going to go. The night went as planned and Maura found that she was as popular as ever, however she drew the line at having sex in the back seat of a car so if her admirer wanted to see her again he would have to book a room for them at a decent hotel. He readily agreed to do just that.

The month's mind Mass for Bob took place on the Thursday evening and there was a good turnout, they were mostly Stephen and Maura's acquaintances; Bob didn't appear to have many friends, which was sad. Sarah went to nursery school on the Friday morning; Maura went to the beauty parlour in readiness for her liaison that night; she had a full pedicure and manicure, which lasted an hour and a half. After a quick shopping trip, Maura collected her daughter from the nursery; she had settled in well but was glad to see her mother. The shopping had consisted of books on interior design and a book for each of her children; Maura wasn't going to look at her books until after the weekend.

On a sudden impulse Maura decided to drive to Waterford to spend the weekend with her parents. Hastily she packed a bag for herself and her two children before phoning her husband to let him know what was happening; unfortunately she didn't give her proposed liaison a second thought; besides which she didn't have a contact number for him. It would take between three to four hours to get to her parents place, which was allowing for stops for the bathroom and one for a hot meal. Maura had rang her parents before setting out just in case they had made plans for the weekend, luckily for her they hadn't, her parents were well used to their daughter's sudden whims and they loved seeing their grandchildren. Sean and Sarah loved their mother's spontaneity, not that they knew it by this name; they called it her funny time, a time when they had adventures and fun. Their journeys were always fun; they sang all their favourite songs and played I-spy games until Sarah fell asleep and Sean fell quiet. Maura glanced in her rear view mirror to make sure her offspring were all right and satisfied that they were she continued the drive to Waterford. They made good time and reached Tramore before 8p.m.; they were given a warm welcome by Maura's parents.

Chapter 5

The weekend in Tramore passed very quickly for them all, they were sorry when the time came for them to go back home. Maura was more than pleased with how it had gone; she now had a good idea about what to do with her spare time. After having discussed the financial details with her parents, and getting a commitment from them to finance it, Maura was going to set up her own interior design company. Her parents thought this would be a great opportunity for her to blossom in her own right, and they had every confidence in her, even if she didn't have any formal qualifications or experience in that field.

The idea had been developing over a few months now. The first time that Maura had thought about it was when she decorated Bob's bedroom, while he was still in hospital. She hadn't physically decorated the room herself, but it was her choice of colour scheme, along with furniture and soft furnishings that won praise from anyone who had seen the room. It had been one of Stephen's employees who had done all the preparation and actual painting under the watchful eye of Maura. Her parents had every faith in her business acumen and although they had, in the past, indulged her; they knew that if Maura put her mind to something she would succeed.

They had kept their discussions till the children were in bed at night, preferring to spend the daytime having fun with the children. Once the children were settled for the night, the adults relaxed with a well-deserved nightcap; then the discussions would start. Maura's parents went through a list of the pros and cons and together they were able to shorten the list of cons and lengthen the list of pros; in this way they were all convinced that an interior design company was a sure fire winner. Maura's parents had made their money by hard work but also by some shrewd investments on the stock market. Her father often quoted the saying 'You have to speculate to accumulate,' but they also taught their daughter to look after her money. Her parents still continued to give her a generous monthly allowance even after setting Stephen up in the painting trade; they made sure that Maura had the controlling interest in the firm, this safe-guarded their investment. Maura wondered what Stephen would think about his wife running her own business. In fairness to Stephen he was easy going and didn't interfere in whatever Maura wanted to do. His wife was strong willed and in the end she would do whatever suited her; this was one of the things that had attracted him to her in the first place.

The journey back to Dublin was uneventful and the Sunday traffic hadn't been too heavy, they reached home at about 7p.m. and were glad to get out of the car to stretch their legs. They had made only one brief stop to take Sarah to the toilet, they were all a bit tired after the weekend and were eager to get to their beds. Maura's mother had packed a large picnic basket, full of treats and goodies for the journey and in fairness there wasn't much in the line of junk food. When Maura saw the size of the basket she burst out laughing, she teased her mother about the amount of food she had packed; they were only going about 105 kilometres. Her mother reminded her that it was better to be prepared as anything could happen, they could encounter heavy traffic or even have a breakdown, which would delay them; this was true so Maura kissed her mother and thanked her for everything. She loved her parents dearly as did her children.

Stephen was pleased to see them home safe and sound and they had an enjoyable hour catching up, the children talked non-stop about their weekend activities and Stephen gave them his full attention. Finally, Maura sent Sean upstairs for his shower and she took Sarah up for a quick wash; Sarah was too sleepy to have a bath and Maura knew she would get overtired if she didn't get to bed soon. Both children were fast asleep within ten minutes of getting into bed. Stephen had poured two brandies for himself and Maura and he was waiting patiently in the lounge when he heard the shower in Maura's en suite running. He knew that Maura was excited about something but she had been very secretive over the phone and had given little away; so naturally he was on tender hooks waiting to find out what she might be planning. At first Stephen thought that Maura might be planning to leave him but then he remembered that she had told him not to worry, that it might even be of benefit to him; he was intrigued.

At last Maura breezed in to the room, she was now wide awake and very animated; it was a long time since he'd seen his wife this excited about anything. He pleaded with her to put him out of his misery, even though her enthusiasm was infectious.

Maura enjoyed having the stage, it gave her a sense of power and a new lease of life; she realised that she had become very set in her ways since her children had come along. Maura told Stephen her plans for the new business venture and Stephen listened without interrupting. When she had finished he remained silent for a few minutes and just stared at his wife before congratulating her on having such a brilliant idea; he was genuinely pleased for her and he could see the possible knock-on benefits for his business.

Over the next few months Maura was busy formulating ideas for the new company, there was a mountain of work to get through and Maura was in her element. She had purchased books on interior design, feng shui, colour charts and carpet books as well as a swatch of various materials and numerous other accoutrements; Maura had filled one of their spare rooms with all the paraphernalia she deemed essential. She had done her homework well and worked tirelessly to get the business up and running; she had acquired an office within 2 kilometres of her home, it was in an ideal location. Maura had been on the lookout for a rental property in the locality and had been disappointed with all of the places she had seen at the beginning. Finally she got a call from a friend of hers telling her about a new property that was coming on to the market in the next few days. Maura wasted no time getting on to the letting agency and she secured the tenancy to the office space straight away; she couldn't believe her good luck. Things were quickly falling in to place and Maura was up to her eyes in contracts and the accompanying paperwork, she loved being kept busy and never once regretted her decision to go with her instincts. She knew exactly what she wanted and that included her choice of staff; Maura had very high standards and she put the interviewees through a tough meeting before deciding who to call back for a second interview. Anyone who was called back was lucky and as far as Maura was concerned they were worth their weight in gold to her, only the best for Maura.

The successful applicants were going to be working in a new and dynamic company and their incentive was a well above average salary. Maura was in her element, she hadn't been this happy since she was a teenager and her children loved this new side to their mother; Stephen had no complaints either. Maura had been too busy for her Friday night escapades, setting up the new business was the only stimulant that she needed right then; she was satisfied with it for the time being.

As the opening date approached Maura became nervous about the venture. A local politician, who was a personal friend, was invited to cut the ribbon and declare 'Home Comforts' officially open for business. The name wasn't the most original but it was the best that Maura could come up with at short notice; her new receptionist happened to ask when the sign for above the door was being erected. This was the one thing that she had forgotten to organise and she hadn't even given a thought to choosing a name for the company, Maura began to panic. There was a mad rush ringing round all the sign writers in the local phone directory, they were extremely lucky to get one who was willing to take on such a rush job. When the sign writer asked Maura to meet him to go through some of the designs for the nameplate she suddenly realised she didn't have a name for the business. The office staff came up with a few suggestions but Maura didn't like any of them; then quite by accident her husband had given her the idea when he said he liked his creature comforts, which Maura amended to 'Home Comforts'. Maura felt this name would do for the time being, and in her mind she thanked her husband for help in solving the dilemma of what to call the business.

Stephen had been very supportive in his own way; he had taken some of the responsibility of looking after their children while Maura was otherwise engaged; he now organised their bedtime routine, which was a big help. Jean played a bigger part in their upbringing; she also stayed late to facilitate the bath time routine and just left Stephen the stories to read when they were tucked up in bed. As far as had been possible, Maura made a point of being at home when the children came home from school and nursery; she also did her best to eat dinner with them each evening. Sean and Sarah offered their advice and Sean actually had a flair for colour coordination, he was very artistic, like his mother. At school this term, Sean's teachers were pleased with his progress in all subjects and he was less disruptive than before; Maura noticed this at home as well, she made a mental note to encourage him. As for Sarah, she had really settled at the nursery, she was like a mother to some of the other children, even those a little older than herself; her key worker had no problem with her at all. Life was really going very well for the Breslin family and Maura expected things to get even better once the business was up and running; she hoped to be able to take on more staff as soon as the jobs started coming in. Maura didn't have long to wait for this to happen and apart from a few teething problems in the very early days everything was going from strength to strength. Maura's parents had come up for the official opening and they were pleasantly surprised at all their daughter had achieved in such a short time; they were very impressed, as was Stephen when he visited the office for the first time. He had never seen this side of his wife's talents before and he wondered why she hadn't taken on a project like this before now.

Stephen knew that this particular endeavour was going to be an enormous success, and he felt a pang of jealousy, which he was quick to banish from his thoughts. Instead he vowed to put in an extra effort in his own business, there was no reason why he shouldn't achieve a similar success; he just had to have more ambition and drive. Since his wife had started this project Stephen's feelings for her had been reawakened but he knew he didn't stand a chance of ever getting back to the way it had been in the early days of their marriage. Still he could live with things the way they were now, which was just as well because Maura had no intention of revisiting that side of their marriage; she'd been there, done that and got the t-shirt. Maura hadn't thought about sex in months, but she didn't anticipate staying celibate for the rest of her life; she still had needs and had once considered investing in a vibrator, but she'd dismissed that preferring the real thing. Maura planned to paint the town red once 'Home Comforts' was established, she talked to her friends often; they kept her up to date with their love lives and exploits, they were looking forward to getting together again and re-establishing their Friday nights 'on the pull'. There was a lot to look forward to in the coming months.

'Home Comforts' was an instant success, partly because there were only a handful of this type of company in the country, and secondly because of the amount of work that Maura put in to it. She gave her heart and soul to make it a success, putting in long hours and taking little out in the way of wages; she worked tirelessly and it was paying off. Within two weeks of opening, Maura had her first job, a newly renovated apartment; owned by a young executive in his thirties. The apartment was in Ballsbridge and the owner wanted Maura to furnish and decorate the apartment to a high standard, he didn't have the time or the inclination to do this himself. He was leaving for Switzerland at the weekend and he would be away for ten days, he intended moving straight in to the apartment on his return; hence the reason for contacting 'Home Comforts'. Maura tried to discuss his personal likes and dislikes and any colour preferences, but the client was quite content to leave everything in her capable hands; she had carte blanche.

Maura's client had heard of something called minimalism which he mentioned might suit his personality that is if Maura thought it would; she, after all was the expert. Yes, Maura thought this a good choice, a clutter free space with simplicity of form and arrangement would be ideal for the young executive.

Maura got to work straight away choosing the right pieces of furniture to give clean simple lines and added just a hint of colour in the accessories; she was very pleased with the final result, she had very good tastes. The apartment was finished on time and her client was delighted with the transformation, he praised Maura's design skills and promised to recommend her to his friends and colleagues. Even when Maura presented him with her bill, which was greatly inflated, he didn't bat an eyelid and in fact he added on a bonus as a means of thanking her for a job well done. Maura was on cloud nine. This she felt was a good omen and she bought champagne for all who had worked on the project, including the office staff.

The next enquiry to 'Home Comforts' was from a newly qualified architect, who unlike the previous client had his own ideas for decorating his office, he wanted to use his office space in conjunction with his passion for astronomy. He wasn't quite sure how to make this work but he thought that between himself and Maura that they'd be able to come up with something suitable, something different.

At first, Maura thought his ideas wouldn't work but after giving it a lot of consideration she came up with an idea that would incorporate his love of the heavens in a down to earth practical working space. There were a few hiccups initially, but this project was also a success, and once again the exorbitant charges were paid without hesitation or question. Maura didn't use her husband's painting and decorating firm for the first few months, as she wanted to get an idea of what services were available in the locality; besides Stephen had other work on. He was still a little peeved not to have been asked, he thought that his wife didn't think he was good enough to do the work. Maura reassured him that this wasn't the case, in reality she didn't want to have to spend too much time with him; though she kept these thoughts to herself. However after a few months and with the work continuing to come in, Maura took a chance and hired some specialist decorators; at the same time she agreed to give Stephen some of the more general work. This seemed to keep everyone happy and there was more than enough work to go round and Maura was able to give Stephen his instructions over the phone. Stephen followed her instructions to the letter, knowing that if he didn't she'd pull rank in his business and he'd be left high and dry. It made sense for them to get along, as they weren't in opposition to each other; quite the opposite in fact. Once they realised this, things got back on an even keel. Maura proved to be a true professional and her business thrived. In the first year of establishing the company she had to employ the only two qualified interior designers in Dublin at that time. After the second year Maura had to advertise for designers in England, if she wanted to keep up with her workload. She was considering opening up another office in Ballsbridge as her business was expanding rapidly, Maura wanted to take advantage of the tax benefits given to businesses at the present time.

Jean had moved in to their home on a temporary basis until such time as 'Home Comforts' required less of Maura's time. The children were growing up fast, Maura hated having so little time with them; but she trusted Jean implicitly and things would be different soon. Sean's grades were improving and Sarah was now in national school and doing well; Sean would be off to secondary school in September, he was looking forward to this. Maura's Friday nights hadn't really got back on track just yet, one of the girls had got engaged and another was going through a messy separation with a custody battle looming. The latter was thinking of going to England to get a divorce, Maura told her that divorce would eventually be brought in, in Ireland, but her friend wasn't prepared to wait for that to happen. So the Friday night group had dwindled to three, and they only met up once a month. Maura felt it was time to bring new blood in to their midst, in the form of the two latest designers to join 'Home Comforts', Holly and Sinead. There were no objections from the other two, so on the Monday morning Maura mentioned to Holly and Sinead that they would be more than welcome to join her and her friends on their Friday night escapades; both new recruits were delighted to have been asked and both accepted the invitation with gratitude. Holly and Sinead had been recruited for the workforce in England and they didn't know anyone in Dublin so the invitation to socialise with their boss was seen as an ideal way to get to meet and make new friends. Maura arranged to meet up with them on the Friday night after first swearing them to secrecy about their antics and activities; what took place outside the office stayed outside the office. Holly and Sinead weren't sure if Maura was serious or not but they agreed to this stipulation. The new group of five got on extremely well and it soon became obvious to the new members why they should keep their private lives private.

Almost three years after the business was well and truly established, the girls went on one of their usual Friday night excursions; they had their regular few drinks before going on to a favourite club. Maura was on her way to the cloakroom when someone tapped her on the shoulder, she was about to give him a mouthful but thought he looked vaguely familiar and cute too. She couldn't quite remember where she might have met him; he was quick enough to tell her that she had stood him up over three years ago. Maura still couldn't quite place him, so he reminded her that she had got him to book a room in a decent hotel one Friday night. Gradually it came back to her and she was impressed that he'd remembered her; she said that she had to go to the toilet, but she'd come back to talk to him afterwards. It came back to her that he was the man she'd passed up a date with to go to Waterford; the weekend she had put her business proposal to her parents. Hmm, he still looked good and she knew that she must have made an impression on him. It wasn't the fact that he'd paid out for a room, which he never used; he didn't look as if he couldn't afford it. Maura teased him and offered to refund the money he was out; he said he'd prefer to be paid in kind. They both knew what he meant and they both knew that it was going to happen. Maura returned to her friends and told them that they'd have to make their own way home as she had a lift, then taking her jacket and bag she said goodnight to them. They all looked in the direction that Maura was headed in and they agreed that he was a bit of all right; none of them would turn him down. Maura broke all her own rules that night by going back to his place without telling anyone his address; Maura prayed that she wouldn't regret it. Larry turned out to be an assistant bank manager who owned his own home, which to Maura's keen eye could do with some serious modernisation; and she was just the right person to do it. They hit it off immediately and Larry said she could put her talents to good use by refurbishing his house; he didn't expect Maura to give him a discount as he had been planning to get a company in to do the majority of the work anyway. How could Maura refuse, she could already see the potential; this was going to be a labour of love for Maura. During her many forays into antique shops and flea markets, Maura had come across several pieces of bric-a-brac and some larger pieces of furniture, which she had purchased on behalf of 'Home Comforts'. She was always on the lookout for unusual items that she would eventually find a home for at some stage.

Larry and Maura's affair continued on Friday nights, she had her own rules regarding affairs. She would only meet him one night a week, and she never gave out either her home address or her home phone number; if this didn't suit her lovers then Maura put an end to the affair straight away. Maura was not prepared to let her affairs encroach on her home life; she had to keep them separate. Larry was happy to go along with this arrangement at the beginning, but six months down the road he began to want more from their relationship. This caused a lot of tension between Maura and himself and he decided that their relationship wasn't going anywhere; so Larry decided to end the affair. This came as a bolt from the blue and Maura was gutted, she wasn't used to being dumped; she was usually the one doing the dumping. There was no way that she could give any more of herself or her time to Larry, if she did it would affect her home life and that wasn't an option. Maura thought that after a while of being apart, Larry would miss her and want her back, but as time went on she knew that this wasn't going to happen. Within a month of the break up, Larry was seeing another woman and three months later he had got engaged and the wedding was planned for that summer. Maura thought that Larry was on the rebound and she felt he was making a big mistake; still she wasn't going to be forced to change her rules. It was upsetting to think that he could have moved on so quickly but that was life. Maura gave the club scene a miss, she knew she was a little too old to act like a teenager; she did still go out with the girls on a Friday night. Of course Stephen hadn't noticed anything different; Maura had always been home in her own bed before anyone got up in the morning.

Sean was now in secondary school and doing well, he was very protective of his younger sister who was seven years old going on seventeen. Sarah was quite precocious and a little spoilt; both parents indulged their children; Maura more so, perhaps to appease her conscience over her affairs. She had overheard her daughter telling her dolls that she was going clubbing and might not be home until the morning, she told her dolls not to tell their daddy. Maura was jolted out of her complacency, she hadn't realised that her children knew what she got up to when she went out on a Friday night. Sarah's role-playing had made it look as if it was normal to have affairs; this wasn't the way that Maura wanted her to grow up. Maura confided in Jean as to what she had witnessed when Sarah was playing with her dolls. Jean tried to reassure her that it wouldn't have a permanent adverse effect on the children and if Maura changed her ways now; the children were still young and impressionable; Maura could turn things around, if she wanted to. This was a turning point in her life and she made a promise to herself to be a better mother and set her children a good example. Life ran smoothly again with Maura's company taking up all of her time, she needed to keep busy both mentally and physically. Stephen was still making an effort to expand his business, he still had some enthusiasm for it, though this could wax or wane as the mood took him. He even believed that he had a happy marriage, albeit sexless; they were still living under the same roof, he must be doing something right by not doing anything. Maybe someday Maura would tell him what he'd done wrong.

Chapter 6

On Sean's thirteenth birthday his parents took him and twelve of his friends to the bowling alley and afterwards to McDonalds, Sarah stayed at home with Jean, preparing a birthday tea; they baked him his favourite chocolate cake and Sarah put thirteen candles on it. Sarah loved her big brother and he always looked out for her; they had some very deep discussions about their parents, they wondered if all families were like theirs. Somehow Sean didn't think that there could be any other families quite like his, none of his mates' parents were like his and he didn't think any of Sarah friends parents were either. Some of Sean's friends were starting to notice girls but not Sean he was still sports mad; girls were a hindrance; they got in the way all the time. Maura was happy enough about this; he had plenty of time to start fancying girls; that's when the trouble would start for sure. Maura felt that she was getting old and she dreaded the day when her little girl, Sarah, grew up and started dating, she didn't think she was going to be able for that; thank God it was a few years off.

Being an only child, Maura was delighted that her children got on so well, they had their rows and disagreements just like other children but they were still very close. Sarah had insisted on staying at home to help Jean to bake Sean's birthday cake, besides she didn't like bowling. For her birthday, she was going to ask her parents to take her to the cinema and she didn't want to go to McDonalds. Sarah wanted a proper birthday party with sandwiches and jelly and ice cream and lots of other treats; she had already discussed the menu with Jean, though her birthday wasn't for another two months. Sarah liked to be organised, she was like her mother in that respect. Stephen thought she was like him, and she was, in her colouring, she had brown eyes like his, but that was the only resemblance. Sarah liked nice clothes and dressing up at weekends, she was very lady like and kept her bedroom neat and tidy; Jean found her a pleasure to mind.

After baking Sean's cake, Sarah went upstairs to her bedroom to get changed for Sean's birthday tea; she was going to help ice the cake when she went back downstairs. Jean was waiting for Sarah to come back down but there was no sign of her after twenty minutes so Jean went up to see what was keeping her. Sarah was as white as a sheet and lying across her bed; she was clutching her stomach and groaning softly. Jean knew she didn't look well and as she went to get the thermometer Sarah threw up all over her bed. Jean felt her forehead and found that she was burning up; she didn't need a thermometer to tell her that the child was very sick. Sarah's pulse was racing and she started to complain of pain in her stomach, before throwing up again. Jean's immediate thought was that Sarah might have appendicitis. She phoned the family doctor and discovered that he was off duty, a recorded message gave the name and phone number of his locum. Jean didn't wait to get the locum she rang 999; she wasn't taking any chances, Sarah's condition was deteriorating rapidly. She told the operator Sarah's symptoms and was told that an ambulance was being despatched as they spoke. Jean then rang Maura's mobile but it was engaged, she knew that Stephen's phone was on the kitchen table; her only hope was that Sean's mobile wouldn't be engaged. Sean's phone rang a few times before he answered it, Jean was beginning to panic; she had to get in touch with Sarah's parents. When Sean answered, Jean told him to give the phone to his mother as she needed to speak to her straight away, Sean did as he was told and Jean told Maura the news about Sarah just as the ambulance pulled up outside. Maura was in shock and unable to think straight, luckily Stephen was able to organise transport home for Sean's friends and he contacted their parents to let them know that their children would be home earlier than expected. Maura was glad to let Stephen take control; he drove them directly to the hospital, where he knew his daughter was being brought. They arrived at the hospital just as the ambulance with Sarah and Jean in it pulled in at A&E. Jean was almost as pale as Sarah. The paramedics had examined Sarah and they were of the opinion that Sarah's appendix was about to rupture if it hadn't all ready done so. They assured Jean that she had been right not to wait for a locum.

Despite logic telling Maura that it was Jean's quick actions, which had saved Sarah's life, she wondered if Jean should have noticed that something was wrong with Sarah sooner. This thought gnawed away at her and she vowed to question Jean about it later. Sarah had to have emergency surgery, which left her extremely ill afterwards; her parents were afraid that she wasn't going to make it. It was seventy-two hours after her surgery before Sarah started to show some improvement. Maura had slept on an armchair beside her bed since she'd been brought in; Stephen went home at night and returned first thing in the morning, bringing Sean with him. He brought a change of clothes for his wife, who showered in her daughter's en suite, and that had been her routine for the last few days. They had a job to get Sean to leave his sister's bedside, and he refused to go to school on the Monday. Maura gave in to him on this occasion she knew he wouldn't settle at school but he would have to go the next day. By the Tuesday evening Sarah was looking and feeling much better, the surgeon said that her temperature was back to normal; she had been given the all clear on her blood test results. She was on a course of antibiotics intravenously, and he wanted her to stay in hospital for at least a week post surgery; she had been a very lucky little girl. Maura questioned him in private about her daughter's sudden onset of appendicitis; Maura still thought that Jean must have missed something on the day that Sarah took ill. The surgeon told Maura that this condition could occur without any symptoms being present beforehand. This allayed Maura's totally unfounded suspicions; she wondered why she had ever doubted Jean who she had known for almost thirteen years. Maura was glad that she hadn't voiced her suspicions to anyone else; Jean especially would be highly offended, and rightly so. Maura didn't know what had come over her, she was an intelligent woman; but these weren't intelligent thoughts that she'd had about Jean.

Stephen had put his wife's crankiness down to her concerns over her daughter's health; he knew it was quite natural, as they had been in shock when they'd first heard of Sarah's illness. Stephen was quite pragmatic, he knew that Jean would keep things ticking over and running smoothly at home; this just left him to organise the work for his lads and to deal with Maura and her mood swings. Maura insisted that Sean return to school on the Wednesday, it was important that he didn't get behind with his schoolwork. There had been many text messages to Maura from her friends and her work colleagues at 'Home Comforts'; all wished Sarah a full and speedy recovery. Sarah had received flowers from the office staff and boxes of chocolates as well as teddy bears of varying sizes; her hospital room was full of gifts from well wishers and personal friends of Maura's.

Jean visited every morning after Sean had gone to school; Sarah always had a great welcome for her; this made Maura feel embarrassed that she'd had any bad thoughts about her. Her conscience was bothering her and she felt slightly uncomfortable around Jean; she considered telling Jean about her feelings. Her change of attitude towards Jean had not gone unnoticed, though Jean put it down to worry and stress over her daughter. Once Sarah had settled down for the night Maura ventured as far as the canteen, which stayed open until 11p.m. each night; she would sit and unwind with a decaf coffee, until it was time to go back to her daughter's room. On the night before Sarah was due to be discharged, Maura was having her usual coffee when she recognised a man who had just walked in; Maura's face lit up as she watched her ex-lover queuing up to pay for his drink.

He looked just as handsome as he had the last time she'd seen him and even now he could still send shivers down her spine. Maura wanted him again, this time it was a real physical longing; she hadn't had sex since the last time she'd been with him, over a year ago. Larry hadn't turned round yet so he hadn't seen her, and Maura was glad that she had put on some perfume and her lipstick, she knew she looked good. She was having a job controlling her urge to go up and throw her arms around him, be cool she told herself; wait for him to come to you. It was just as well that she didn't approach him, because he wasn't alone; his wife, Julie, was waiting at a corner table for him to join her.

Maura's face dropped and her heart sank when she realised that any thoughts of picking up where they left off were now no longer possible. The disappointment she felt was palpable and tears stung her eyes; she averted her gaze so no one would see. It hurt to see Larry and his wife together, it served as a reminder that her own marriage was loveless; jealousy was rearing its ugly head, an emotion that Maura hadn't experienced before; well not as strong as this time. While trying not to look in Larry's direction; Maura knew for certain that she'd have to do something about her love life, or lack of it. Maura missed male company, and she was lonely. At that moment Julie left the canteen and headed in the direction of the wards; she was obviously going back to visit whoever she was here to see. This was a chance for Maura to reacquaint herself with Larry who was sitting on his own now; she walked across to his table and feigned surprise at seeing him. Larry looked uncomfortable and glanced across the canteen to make sure his wife had left; he didn't want to have to introduce his wife to his ex lover. Maura didn't get the response she was hoping for from Larry, he was nervous and continued to watch the door in case his wife should return. He told Maura that they were visiting Julie's mother, who had emphysema; from years of smoking forty cigarettes a day. The emphysema had put a strain on her heart and was causing her trouble breathing; she was on oxygen since being admitted yesterday, they were very concerned about her condition. Maura wasn't the least bit interested in the condition of Larry's mother in law, but she feigned concern. Larry asked Maura how her family were and he was glad to hear that Sarah had made a good recovery and was going home the next day. He was the first to make a move to leave, he said Julie would be wondering what was keeping him; he said it had been nice seeing Maura but that he had to go. Maura, being Maura made a sarcastic remark about who ruled the roost; Larry told her in no uncertain terms that sarcasm was the lowest form of wit. Maura was speechless, Larry had never spoken to her like that before, and she'd been joking about ruling the roost; maybe she'd hit a nerve. Larry was still talking, he was saying how much in love he was with his wife; they had an equal partnership based on love and mutual respect for each other. Me think he doth protest too much, thought Maura; who had been stung by his outburst. She was determined to find out just what state his marriage was in; of course she could always ask his wife, but as Sarah was going home in the morning Maura was unlikely to see her again; besides, Larry wouldn't like it if she did. Maura racked her brain to come up with a plausible excuse to visit Julie's mother, she thought she might be able to glean something from her as regards her daughter's marriage. It was easy to find the women's ward and then to find Julie's mother, Larry had said she was on oxygen, which narrowed it down to two ladies. One was too old, that left Julie's mother in the bed nearest the door, Maura was laden down with bottles of minerals; her excuse to talk to the woman sitting up in the bed, was that her daughter had too many and she was going home in the morning. Mary Mangan, Julie's mother thanked Maura for her thoughtfulness, and Maura took the opportunity to sit down beside her bed. Maura had just got to the shop before it closed at 9p.m., to buy the bottles of minerals; it was the best excuse she could come up with in such a short period of time. Mary thought that Maura was very friendly but she was tired and would have preferred to go to sleep, she didn't want to appear rude and it was difficult talking with the oxygen mask on. Maura told Mary about her daughter and said what a blessing a daughter was; Mary agreed and said that her Julie who was an only child was a godsend. Maura asked if Julie had any children herself, Mary said that she had only been married for a year and there was plenty of time for them yet. Maura had the audacity to ask Mary if her daughter was happily married, after all maybe that was why she hadn't any children. Mary couldn't believe that a total stranger was casting doubts on her daughter's relationship with her husband. Mary was extremely upset but told Maura that her daughter and son-in-law were very happily married; and she asked Maura to leave, she was tired, which though true wasn't the reason she wanted Maura to go. Mary was actually a bit frightened of Maura and she suspected that she had ulterior motives for coming to talk to her; what those motives might be she couldn't fathom. Maura was quite put out that she'd been asked to leave but she didn't argue with the woman, and of course she would say her daughter was happily married, she wouldn't tell a stranger that there were problems in the marriage. There was always the direct route, Maura remembered that she still had Larry's mobile number and decided that she'd give him a call in a day or so; to invite him out for a drink or something else. Maura smiled to herself, there was more than one way to skin a cat, so the saying went, and there was more than one way to get into Larry's trousers; Maura wasn't giving up that easily.

Chapter 7

Sarah was excited to be going home from hospital, she'd missed being with her family, and she missed Jean's cooking. Some of her school friends had visited her in hospital, they thought she was lucky to have time off from school; and they looked enviously at her presents, especially the boxes of chocolates piled high on her locker. Maura would be glad to have her back home, then they could get back to a normal routine, she had some serious thinking to do when things settled down. She would go back to work on a part-time basis over the next few weeks, Sarah wouldn't be going back to school for another fortnight, and she wouldn't be taking part in P.E. for at least six weeks; until she got the go ahead from her doctor. An appointment had been made for her to return to the outpatients department in a month's time, for a general check up and to monitor her progress. After the checkup, Maura expected to be able to return to work full time, and she was looking forward to it.

Since her disastrous attempt to befriend Julie's mother, Maura had become sullen and dispirited, she knew she'd made a bloody mess of things; and she could kick herself for her tactlessness. God knows what Larry would say when he heard what she'd done, she could just picture him now; he would not be happy. That Mary Mangan one was sure to tell her daughter about the inquisitive visitor she'd had, and Julie was sure to mention it to Larry; Maura was certain that he'd know that it was her, he'd also know the reason she'd been questioning Mary. All in all Maura had made a big mistake in how she had tried to get back with Larry, and she acknowledged that if the shoe was on the other foot she wouldn't want anything to do with her either. Now what Maura needed was a new plan of action, but it must be well thought out and not just something done on the spur of the moment. Maura was going to take her time and think things through before going off again half cocked; and in the meantime she had to start thinking about work.

'Home Comforts' had run smoothly while Maura was absent from work, her staff were very competent, which was why they had been employed in the first place. There were a few minor things for Maura to deal with but nothing urgent. Both offices were very busy and the phones were constantly ringing, and the jobs were coming in daily; there was no doubt that Maura had judged the market well. She thought that if she put as much effort into getting her love life back on track, that she'd be doing well in that department too. Sarah was back on form again after her appendectomy, she was bored being at home and longed to get back to school. Her teacher had sent home schoolwork that she had missed while she was in hospital and then at home recuperating there was no point her slipping behind the rest of her classmates.

Stephen had been back at work full time since Sarah had come home from hospital, and just as well that he was, his young lads had been slacking off during the few days he'd been away. They hadn't made much progress on the basement flat, which they should have finished, or almost finished painting by now. Stephen would have to crack the whip, he wasn't likely to make any profit on the job at this rate, and he also had a backlog of work to get through for Maura who didn't like being kept waiting. The weather wasn't being too kind to him either, he had quite a few outdoor jobs to do but he supposed that there was no point worrying about that; he couldn't do anything about the weather. Stephen wouldn't lose any sleep over such things; he wasn't likely to develop an ulcer either.

Jean was glad that Maura's mood swings had passed; she was in better form since Sarah had come home from hospital and the whole family seemed none the worse for their tribulations. Maura seemed unnaturally calm, almost as if she was biding her time; waiting for something momentous to happen. Jean couldn't begin to imagine what that 'something' might be. She felt she was getting a little too old for this job, she loved the family, but they were hard work; little Sarah's recent hospitalisation had affected her deeply. Jean had been having nightmares since Sarah's almost fatal event, and the events of that day played over and over again in her dreams; sometimes the ending didn't have a happy outcome. Jean also wondered if she should have spotted something in Sarah's behaviour that might have been an indication that her appendix was about to rupture. Maura had been very supportive, and she assured her that the surgeon had said Sarah's appendix had ruptured spontaneously; so there was no way of either foreseeing it or preventing it from happening. It had been Jean's quick actions that had saved Sarah's life, for that Maura would be forever in her debt; this was a complete turn around from what she had originally been thinking. At night when the children were asleep in bed, Maura settled herself with a drink and tried to come up with a solution to her problem; namely how to seduce Larry, Maura really thought that if she applied herself to the task in hand she'd succeed. She remembered the day that Larry had called off their affair; he had said it was because he wanted more from her; that surely had to mean something. He couldn't have just stopped loving her that quickly, Larry wasn't like that. Maura couldn't come up with any plan to get Larry back, so she decided to try the direct approach; she called him on his mobile. It had been two weeks since she'd seen him at the hospital and she hadn't stopped thinking about him, and maybe he was thinking about her; at least this is what Maura hoped was happening. Once again she got a frosty reception from him, he wanted to know what she'd been playing at; visiting his mother-in-law. Julie's mother had described Maura to a T, and though Julie didn't have a clue who she was, Larry did. His mother-in-law was suspicious and she never took her eyes off him while she told them about her unwanted visitor and the personal questions she'd asked regarding Julie and Larry's marriage. Larry was livid, he couldn't believe her audacity. Maura told Larry that she was just trying to be friendly, but he wasn't convinced; he asked her why she was calling him now. Maura said she was enquiring about Mary, his mother-in-law, it was the only thing she could come up with after his tirade. She was sure that she hadn't been very convincing but what the hell, she hadn't thought it through before making the call; if she had she'd have come up with something better. Larry informed her that his mother-in-law had died five nights ago, and he'd prefer it if she didn't contact him again.

Maura hadn't expected that, but he was probably grieving for his mother-in-law, though why; she couldn't fathom. If the old Biddy had warned Julie about Maura, then there wasn't any point worrying about it; 'que sera sera'. Maura thought that Larry might be annoyed with her for being insensitive; she never used to be like that; not when she'd been seeing him. She wasn't giving up on him that easily, she would call him again in a few days, and he'd probably be in better humour then. Maura decided she needed a night out with the girls and so she made arrangements to meet that Friday night, she wanted a little harmless fun; she wasn't looking for company. Maura enjoyed flirting with the men in the pub, she wanted to find out if she was still attractive to them; her confidence had taken a beating when Larry had been so dismissive of her charms at the hospital. She seriously wondered if she'd lost her pulling powers, but the attention she received from the men in the pub left her in no doubt that they still found her attractive.

On the Sunday, Maura and Stephen took their children to the circus, Sean loved the animals, though the thought of them being caged didn't go down well with him, Sarah loved the acrobats and high wire acts. They had an enjoyable afternoon and went on to a restaurant for dinner. Sarah's appetite was still poor since having the surgery, and Maura made a mental note to get a tonic at the chemist for her. Maura went in to the office early on the Monday morning, she had a few phone calls that she wanted to make, in private; she didn't want any of the girls from the office to overhear her conversation. She needn't have worried on that score, as soon as Larry answered his phone and heard Maura's voice he hung up. Maura pressed the redial button and waited for him to answer again; she'd thought that maybe he didn't recognise her voice, as there was a lot of crackling and interference on the line; that must be it. Larry answered again and he was absolutely fuming, he'd heard her all right, he just didn't want to talk to her. If Maura rang him again he threatened to call the guards, he said she was to stop bothering him.

Bothering him; Maura didn't bother people, what was wrong with him? Maura wasn't bothering anyone; she must have caught him at a bad time, she'd let him cool down and call him in a day or two. She wondered if he still worked at the same branch in Stillorgan, it would only take a quick phone call to verify that. Maura made the call and yes he was still assistant manager but he wasn't at his desk right now, Maura could leave a message if she wanted to and he'd get back to her as soon as possible; Maura declined to leave a message, preferring instead to ring back later. She was happy now, she knew where he lived and where he worked and it would be easy for her to bump in to him whenever she wanted to. Just as she'd finished her calls the office staff started to arrive, they were surprised to find their boss there before them, Maura usually dropped the children off at school first, before coming in to the office. They had noticed a change in Maura's behaviour of late, she was distant and her mind wasn't fully on the job; there were times when she was miles away and didn't hear what was being said to her. This was so unlike Maura, she'd always been professional and didn't stand fools gladly; it must be the strain she was under since Sarah had been in hospital, that's the only conclusion they could come to. Holly and Sinead were annoyed at the office staff for discussing their boss's behaviour so openly; this was disrespectful and uncalled for. Secretly, Holly and Sinead were a bit worried about Maura's mental health, she was definitely behaving strangely, and sometimes they heard her muttering to herself about sorting someone called Julie out. Neither designer knew of anyone called Julie, she must be someone from Maura's past; at least that's what they thought. Maybe they should talk to Maura and see if anything was bothering her; or maybe they should talk to Stephen, he'd have a better idea if there were something wrong. The girls decided to let things rest for the moment, they'd keep an eye on their friend and watch out for her for the time being; there was no point rushing in where fools feared to tread.

Things weren't going quite as Maura wanted them to go, despite her persistence, Larry still wasn't softening to her approaches. In the last three months, Maura had rang Larry either on his mobile or at the bank every second day. At the bank, he had been able to have his calls screened, that is until Maura became more devious; calls to his mobile were a different kettle of fish, she left him with no alternative but to change his phone. This was a great inconvenience for him but for the present it solved one problem. Larry had yet to tell his wife about Maura's constant phone calls, and the longer he left it the harder it became, it might look as if he'd been hiding something; which he wasn't. He should have told Julie about his ex when he bumped in to her, at the time when her mother was in hospital; of course that would have been the sensible thing to do. Now that Julie had just found out that she was eight weeks pregnant Larry didn't want anything to jeopardise her chances of carrying their baby to full term; Julie had miscarried on two previous occasions, she didn't need any stress in her life right now. On the last occasion that he'd spoken to Maura, he told her that if she didn't stop phoning him he would have to go to the guards; now it was looking extremely likely that he'd have to, this would be a last resort.

Another way might be to meet her face to face, then he could explain about his wife being pregnant and her miscarriages; appeal to Maura's better nature. If only he hadn't got involved with her in the first place, but it had been good, Maura was an experienced lover; she made him feel like an Adonis. They had a lot of good times, which were being eroded by Maura's unreasonable behaviour and refusal to let go of the past.

Larry made a promise to sort this out one way or another, and if that meant seeing Maura then so be it. He went in to work on the Monday morning with every intention of taking her phone call, however, he was no sooner there when his wife phoned; she was having pains in her stomach and feared that she was losing the baby. Larry told her to ring for an ambulance to get her to the maternity hospital immediately; he would meet her there as soon as he could. He drove as fast as possible, just keeping within the speed limit, Julie had just arrived a few minutes before him; she was being examined by an obstetrician so he'd just have to wait and see what was happening. All thoughts of Maura were banished from his head, Julie and his baby were his only concerns, and he found himself praying for the first time in years, that Julie wouldn't lose the baby. It seemed to take forever for the examination to finally end, after which time the obstetrician explained why Julie had experienced the cramps, and advising that she be admitted to hospital for the duration of her pregnancy.

Julie would require total bed rest for the next six and a half to seven months, even with that there was still no guarantee that she wouldn't lose the baby during that time. Julie and Larry just held each other's hands, they were too upset and scared to say anything, it would take a while to sink in. The doctor said she'd come back later when Julie was settled in the ward and she'd explain things in more detail then. Julie told Larry that she was sorry; she felt a failure for not being able to give him the baby he wanted so badly, she started sobbing and buried her head in her hands. Larry told her that he loved her no matter what happened and he'd still love her no matter what; Julie shouldn't give up so easily, she hadn't lost the baby yet.

Julie was admitted to the antenatal ward, and Larry stayed with her until the obstetrician had come back to see her and explain in more detail why bed rest was essential. The doctor had said that Julie's scan had revealed that she had a medical condition called placenta praevia, which basically meant that the placenta was low down in her uterus and blocking the birth canal; it was a serious cause of concern, bed rest was about the only thing that would, hopefully, stop Julie from losing the baby. Larry found it hard to take it all in but Julie seemed a little more at ease, after all, the doctor didn't say that she would lose the baby; she just said that she might lose it. The next seven months were going to be the longest ever for Julie and Larry, he was going to find it very lonely without his wife's company every night. It would be worth the sacrifices if it meant they'd have a baby at the end of it, that's the thing they'd have to keep telling themselves to get through it. Larry went outside the hospital to make a few phone calls, one of them was to his secretary at the bank who would be anxious to hear how Julie was; he explained briefly what had been said and finished by saying he was going to be away from the bank for the rest of the day. Larry felt a little more optimistic as he headed back to the ward and he needed to keep cheerful for Julie's sake. They talked for more than an hour and by the time Larry was leaving they were both in a buoyant frame of mind.

Julie didn't expect her husband to come back that night, she wanted him to get some rest and she'd do the same. Larry said he'd see how things went, but he knew he'd be there that night and every other night while his wife was in hospital; he was the only family she had now.

As he headed home he realised he was hungry, he hadn't eaten since breakfast, it would be easier for him to eat out that evening rather than cooking for himself; he'd go to The Haven, a steakhouse, which was on his route to the hospital. The house seemed unnaturally quiet when he was in the bedroom packing some things for his wife, he sat down on their double bed and cried silent tears; he felt exhausted. He had to pull himself together and stop wallowing in self-pity, Julie needed him to be strong and in control; otherwise she would go to pieces. Larry took Julie's pretty nightdresses and her toiletries and packed a small bag; he put in one of her books from the bedside locker and went downstairs to switch the answering machine on. On his way to the restaurant he stopped off at the florists and bought an enormous bunch of roses, he then drove to The Haven where he enjoyed a 12 oz T-bone steak. Julie was sleeping when he got to the hospital but she woke up as soon as he reached her bedside, she was so pleased that he'd come in again, that she started crying. Larry put his arms around her, and whispered endearments in her ear; then he told her that everything would be O.K.; they would come out of this with their beautiful baby, and they'd be great parents. Julie smiled at her husband and felt that she was the luckiest woman alive; she wanted to have his baby so badly that it hurt. Larry didn't stay too long with Julie, she was tired from all the tests she'd had that afternoon; he would call in to see her during his lunch-hour, the next day. Julie didn't want him coming in during the day, he had enough to do at work without wasting his lunch-hour on visiting her; she insisted that he wait till the evening. Larry was secretly relieved not to be driving across town in the lunchtime traffic; life was stressful enough without that.

The next day was a busy one at work, Larry had one meeting before lunch and a further two in the afternoon; a third had been scheduled but Larry got his secretary to defer it until the following afternoon. He hadn't recognised the name in his appointment book, but he hoped whoever she was that she wouldn't mind waiting another day. Maura did mind waiting but his secretary had told her that he apologised sincerely for any inconvenience that this may have caused, so how could she be annoyed at him; he didn't know that it was her he was due to see, she'd given a false name. Maura was sure that if she'd given her real name that Larry wouldn't see her, she didn't like being sneaky but he didn't give her much choice; she only wanted to talk to him, she wouldn't bite him. Larry visited his wife that evening before picking up a take-away meal from the local Chinese restaurant, he was going to have to start cooking for himself; he couldn't live on take-aways for the next seven months. Julie had been much cheerier when he saw her that evening and had made friends with the other women in the ward; they all had their own problems, which Julie didn't go in to. It made it easier for Larry if his wife was content, then he didn't feel guilty leaving her there; he couldn't imagine being confined to a hospital bed for so long, he'd go crazy. He was ready for an early night in bed; he had a busy schedule for the rest of the week and wanted to be in tip-top form for those meetings. The morning was bright and sunny and Larry had slept soundly the previous night, which boded well for the day ahead. Larry had brought a sandwich with him to save time at lunchtime; he would eat at his desk and that way he could get through some of the paperwork piling up on his desk. His first appointment after lunch was with one of the managers from another branch, they had a few projects in the pipeline and this meeting was just to iron out a few minor hiccups that had occurred. Their meeting was over within an hour, leaving Larry time to phone his wife before seeing his next client; Julie was happy enough, and each day was a day nearer to having their baby.

Larry loved his wife so much and he loved how she always picked herself up after a fall. Larry's intercom buzzed, his next client was waiting to see him; he told his secretary to send in Mrs Christie as he was ready to see her. Larry stood up to shake hands with Mrs Christie and for one dreadful moment he thought he was going to fall over; the said Mrs Christie was none other than Maura Breslin.

Maura laughed at Larry's shocked expression, his mouth was hanging open and he hadn't been able to say a word since she'd walked in. She liked to make an entrance and this was as good as she could come up with, now she had Larry's full attention.

'Did you like the name I chose? Mrs Christie, get it, Agatha Christie as in mystery writer,' said Maura to a stunned Larry. Larry still hadn't been able to speak; he sat down and looked over at Maura who was grinning like a Cheshire cat.

'What the hell do you want Maura, what are you playing at?' said Larry finding his voice at last.

Maura smiled sweetly before telling him that she missed his company on those long Friday nights, they should never have split up; they were good for each other.

Larry couldn't believe what he was hearing, this wasn't the woman he'd fallen madly in love with some time ago; this person sitting in front of him was unhinged, this was madness. Larry listened to Maura's ramblings about missing him and wanting him, and saying that they'd be good for each other; there was no stopping her, so he let her have her say before telling her it was never going to happen. Larry told Maura that he didn't want her, he was happy with Julie and she had to get over it and leave him alone; he regretted ever having been involved with her, he couldn't deal with this harassment.

Eventually he managed to persuade Maura to leave, it hadn't been easy, he'd had to promise to think it over and ring her on Friday. He had no intention of thinking anything over; he had to contact the guards. This was a form of stalking and Maura had really frightened Larry, he didn't know she could be so devious or scheming; God knows what she was capable of, and he couldn't risk her finding out that Julie was in hospital; she'd plague him constantly if she knew and he'd never get rid of her.

Larry left the bank shortly after he'd managed to get Maura to go, he didn't want to ring the Gardai from his office; he'd do that from home, she'd left him no choice.

The Garda that he spoke to was sympathetic and suggested that he contact his solicitor and get him to send her a letter advising her to cease communicating with him; if this didn't have the desired effect, Larry should get back to them and they'd take it from there.

When Maura got the solicitor's letter she was livid, it had arrived at 'Home Comforts' two days after she'd been to see Larry. The letter told her in no uncertain terms that she was to refrain from contacting their client; either in person or by telephone, they strongly advised her that they would take a very dim view of things if she ignored this warning.

Warning, thought Maura, what were they warning her about, was Larry such a wimp that he had to threaten her with a solicitor's letter? Maura didn't like being threatened. She'd back off for now as she needed to concentrate on her business for the time being, she'd been neglecting it of late; Larry would keep.

Chapter 8

Maura had worked hard to build up her interior design business but if she didn't buckle down and do some real work she could end up losing it all. She knew that she had been neglecting her company of late and maybe the solicitor's letter would serve as a wake up call for her. It seemed so long since she'd actually done any real work and her staff could do with a bit of a shake up as well as herself. Maura's parents were coming up to Dublin in a few months' time and she wanted to have everything running smoothly; she wanted her parents to be proud of her, and what she had achieved. If she acted now she could get things moving again in an upward direction, the business needed new blood to put the spark back into it. Her designers were the best, but they needed to come up with some new ideas; there was a lot of competition in the interior design business, which hadn't been there when Maura started out. She didn't think that the other companies were a real threat, as she had earned a good a reputation for her own company; she'd made a name for herself.

Sean had had his fifteenth birthday, and already he was six feet tall; he was popular with both the boys and girls at his school. This last year had seen his interest in girls evolving and Sarah teased him, good-naturedly about the amount of time he spent in front of the mirror. Sarah too, was growing up fast and she would be ten years old later on in the year; Maura couldn't believe how much her children had grown this past year.

Stephen was putting the weight back on again and he'd stopped going swimming and to the gym months ago; and his bad eating habits were back and as bad as they'd ever been. Maura didn't even seem to notice, they had drifted even further apart, if that was possible; she didn't know why they were still living together. She supposed that they just couldn't be bothered to get a legal separation; she was as much to blame for this as Stephen. Poor Stephen, thought Maura, what had he ever done to be saddled with her, a total bitch, who only ever thought of herself? Lately she hadn't even had time for her children, what must they think of her; she used to be so together, so organised and so much fun to be with. Maura couldn't remember the last time they had any fun together or when they'd last done anything together; that had to change, a lot of things had to change. Jean was more of a mother to Sean and Sarah than Maura was, and they turned to Jean and not her when they needed anything. Maura could soon rectify that if she spent more quality time with them, she promised herself to do just that, and turn over a new leaf. Maura did her best and this new phase lasted for several months, the Breslin children gave it a cautious welcome; Stephen didn't see any difference in her behaviour; it didn't affect him directly.

Maura hadn't entirely put Larry out of her mind, but she did heed the solicitor's letter, she would be mortified if her family ever found about it; not that she would ever accept that she had been a stalker, which was bullshit. The temptation to phone her ex was still there, only now she had to control that urge. Instead Maura put all her efforts into 'Home Comforts' and it was paying dividends, and it gave her something solid to focus on. Maura had hired another interior designer, Ciara, who was Irish, and had been trained in Ireland; she was just what Maura's company needed. Ciara had lots of interesting ideas in design and she had completed a course in feng shui, a philosophy concerning the flow of energy in a room or building and governing the placement and arrangement of furniture and accessories to bring good fortune. Maura had heard of feng shui but she didn't profess to understand it, however, it appeared to be building in popularity; which could only be of benefit to her company, having someone who did know about it. Holly and Sinead really liked Ciara, she was definitely going to be an asset to 'Home Comfort', and they told Maura that they thought she'd made a good choice by taking her on. Maura was pleased with herself for taking Ciara on, she was bubbly and outgoing, and this was going to be her first job since leaving college. Anyway it wouldn't hurt to take her on on a trial basis, Ciara was happy with that arrangement; she was confident that she would be kept on after her trial period was up. Maura had just the job for her latest employee, Stephen had just finished painting the inside of two basement flats and 'Home Comforts' had been given the job to furnish them in a contemporary style; this was to be Ciara's first test. Maura had to give her designers a relatively free hand, otherwise they would move on to other companies, and she couldn't afford to let hers go; they were possibly the most experienced in Ireland, and by far the best. Ciara showed Maura some of the materials she was going to use for the soft furnishings, and Maura was impressed; Ciara had great tastes, and hopefully that would continue in the furniture department. It did. Maura was on to a winner with Ciara and within a short period of her starting to work for her she was in demand; with clients asking for her by name. Her work was getting recognition, and 'Home Comforts' was going to reap the benefits; it just took word of mouth to make or break a designer's name. Ciara was going to go to the top in her profession, and Maura was taking the credit for giving her her first brief. Things began to shape up nicely in Maura's life, the relationship with her children improved and she seemed to have settled down again; she no longer obsessed about her love life, or Larry.

Maura's parents were looking forward to their trip up to Dublin at the weekend; they were planning on staying for a fortnight, before flying out to Egypt for a cruise down the Nile. They had hoped to persuade their daughter and grandchildren to join them, but Maura said she'd prefer not to take them out of school during term. Sean and Sarah did everything they could to persuade their mother to change her mind, but she would not be moved, Maura promised to take them away on holiday in June when the school term was over. There was no use in them continuing to press her, she had made up her mind and that was that. Jean was busy spring-cleaning, which wasn't really necessary, but she liked everything to be in tip-top order for the arrival of Maura's parents. They were lovely people and they treated Jean more like family than an employee of their daughter, they constantly reminded Maura and Stephen how lucky they were to have her. On the Friday afternoon, Maura finished work early; she was excited about her parents visit and wanted to be at home when they arrived. She hadn't seen them for almost four months, the longest time ever, she'd meant to go down to see them a month ago but she just didn't get round to it. They did talk often on the phone but it wasn't the same as in person, Maura was so looking forward to showing them around 'Home Comforts', she felt sure they'd be proud of her. Maura stopped off at the patisserie to buy her father's favourite Danish pastries, he had a sweet tooth, which his wife said would lead to him developing diabetes; they both laughed saying, if that didn't kill him something else would. It was a long-standing joke between father and daughter, and Maura smiled to herself when she remembered it. She knew that her father would be expecting the pastries; Maura always bought them for him when he came to stay with them. She drove the rest of the way home listening to the traffic report, hoping her parents didn't get caught up in the heavy weekend traffic. Maura had talked to her mother that morning and she said they would be leaving Waterford before lunchtime, in that way they would miss any rush hour traffic, Maura could expect them in time for tea. Stephen too, was looking forward to their visit, his father-in-law, Jack, was good company and Rita was all right in her own way; he didn't think she liked him. She probably didn't, seeing as he got her little girl pregnant out of wedlock, she knew they hadn't been sleeping together for years, Maura had told her. Still, she wasn't the worst in the world, and they had set him up in business after he'd married Maura; they were only going to be there for two weeks, so that wasn't too bad. Maura reached home at 2p.m. and asked Jean if there had been any calls for her, she was thinking that her mother might have rang to say they were on the road; Jean hadn't taken any calls and she had been there all morning. Maura took a quick shower and checked that the spare room was ready for her parents; she had bought a bouquet of flowers to brighten their room, flowers always cheered her up and her mother liked fresh flowers in the home. Jean had a fresh pot of coffee made and

Maura and herself sat down and enjoyed a cup and caught up on the general gossip. Half an hour later Stephen arrived home and was despatched to his room to take a shower before the in-laws arrived; and for once he didn't protest at being told what to do. Maura debated calling her parents on their mobile, but decided against it on the grounds that they didn't have a hands-free connection in their car; and they'd be better off without a phone distracting them. Stephen was asking Maura what time she thought they'd arrive when their doorbell rang and he went to answer it; Maura could hear the strange voices and wondered who it was.

Stephen walked back to the kitchen, followed by the two Garda who had come to tell Maura the tragic news; her parents had been killed in a head-on collision involving a truck and their car. Maura fell in to a dead faint and was caught by one of the Gardai, before she hit the floor. Stephen and Jean had just stood there, unable to take in what they'd heard. When Maura came round she let out an agonising shriek that went through Stephen; he wasn't sure what to do, but one of the Gardai advised getting Maura's doctor to come round. She would probably need some sedation after the shock she'd received; the gardai asked if there was anything else they could do. Stephen thanked them, but for what he wasn't sure. As the Gardai were leaving they asked Stephen if he or his wife would go down to the hospital mortuary later that day; to formally identify the two bodies. Maura, though in shock could hear what was being said and screamed at the guards that if anyone was going to identify her parents it would be her. Jean had managed to phone Maura's doctor and he was on his way over, there was another thing that had to be organised and that was to collect the children. Jean volunteered to do this, she wouldn't tell them about the tragedy that had occurred; that was a job for their parents to do, she wouldn't have been able to find the right words, not that there were any right words. Suddenly everything had changed and their lives would never be the same again.

Dr Holmes arrived just as Jean was heading out to collect the children, he stopped to have a quick word with her; he knew how much she had thought of Maura's parents, they had been his patients until they'd moved out of Dublin. He found Maura busying herself in the kitchen; she was quite calm and accepted his condolences with a quiet dignity. They talked for almost twenty minutes about the tragic death of her parents, Dr Holmes advised Maura to accept his suggestion of taking a mild tranquilliser; it wouldn't stop her functioning, it was just to help with the anxiety she might experience, over the coming days. Maura refused, saying she needed a clear head to make the funeral arrangements for her parents; Dr Holmes couldn't force her to take the drugs that had to be her decision. Maura told Stephen that she would tell the children about their grandparents' death, and then she wanted him to take her down to their local hospital to identify her parents. Stephen agreed to do whatever she asked, he couldn't believe how calm she appeared to be; inevitably she was going to come down to earth with an unmerciful jolt. The best that Stephen could do was to be there to try to cushion the blow when it came, he knew what it was like to lose your parents, and this was going to be harder for Maura; she'd idolised hers. The next few months would be the hardest but Maura was a strong woman, she would get through it; of that Stephen had no doubt. Jean's car was just pulling into the driveway as Dr Holmes drove away, and Sean and Sarah asked Jean who was sick; but before she had time to answer Maura appeared at the front door, saving Jean from having to answer.

It was a sombre household that evening, with Sarah being inconsolable and Sean unable to show his emotions; Jean felt that their whole lives had been turned upside down; she wasn't sure how they'd ever cope with this, it was the end of an era.

Maura arrived with Stephen to identify the bodies of her parents at the hospital morgue, she was calm and didn't flinch at the sight of their bodies, which were badly bruised and cut. Maura cradled her mother's head in her arms; she asked her mother to forgive her for not being able to take her home straight away, she'd bring her home as soon as they let her. Her father had taken the full force of the impact, his head had almost been severed from his body; the mortuary staff had done the best they could under the circumstances, a post-mortem had been performed, there was little else they could do until the identification had taken place. Maura asked the attendant to look after her mother and father until she could bring them home, he nodded silently; this was always the hardest part of his job, meeting the relatives of the deceased. Stephen's heart was breaking to see his wife in so much pain, it was almost unbearable; and knowing that there was nothing he could do to ease that pain. So far Maura hadn't shed a tear, and Stephen didn't think it was a good omen; not that he was an expert on the grieving process, but he had been through it himself.

Maura insisted on waking her parents for two nights, she wanted to keep them with her for as long as possible; her explanation was that there would be so many people wanting to pay their respects that one night wouldn't be enough. Stephen had tried reasoning with her, saying it would be too stressful on the children having so many people traipsing through their home. Maura gave him one of her withering looks and uttered just one word; tough. Stephen went to his children and explained how upset their mother was and that they'd need to be extra loving towards her; she was hurting so much that she wasn't thinking straight. He tried to explain, as simply as possible, what would be happening over the coming days. Sean had said very little since the accident, he spent most of his time in his bedroom listening to music on his iPod. Sarah however was quite distraught and had hardly stopped crying since the death of her grandparents; she refused to go into the lounge, where her grandparents were laid out. They were laid out in two identical caskets, side by side, and Maura was never far away from them. Stephen was dreading the moment when the caskets would have to be closed; he knew that this would be heartbreaking for his wife, he was afraid of what she might do. Jean had stayed with the family since the news had come through about the accident; she had kept a buffet going from morning to night and even through the night. There was food available, for anyone who wanted it, twenty-four hours a day. Jean organised everything from hot soup and snacks to the large tea urn, which was constantly in use throughout the wake; she made sure that there was enough alcohol of every description to suit every taste. She had anticipated every possible request, she never closed her eyes for the entire duration of the wake, and she also did her best to make sure that the children weren't left on their own too long. Stephen had been a great help, he had been there to speak to everyone who had come through their front door to pay their respects. Maura had organised the undertakers, who in turn had taken over the arrangements; including the death notices and announcements. Once Maura had contacted the undertakers, she left everything else that had to be done to Stephen and Jean; she didn't want to waste any more time away from her parents. Maura needed this time with her mother and father, and no one was going to take it away from her. The local curate arrived to say some prayers for the deceased and then it was time to close the caskets, Maura asked for five minutes alone with her parents, and Stephen ushered everybody out of the lounge. He wished that Sarah had said her goodbyes but no amount of gentle persuasion would entice her to go into the lounge. Stephen was afraid that she would regret her decision in a few years time, but he couldn't force her to say goodbye if she didn't want to. Maura came out from the lounge and gave a nod to the undertaker to let him know that he could do his job now.

All eyes were on Maura to see how she would react to the removal of the caskets bearing the bodies of her parents; she remained dignified, and held her head high, just like her parents would want her to.

Maura was numb, she wished she could just curl up and die like her parents; this just wasn't fair, why her family. Why?

For the next two days everyone was watching and waiting for Maura to break down, even Stephen thought she would show some emotion when the caskets were lowered in to their graves; she didn't have any expression on her face that in itself was scary. Stephen was planning on talking to Dr Holmes, after the funeral, about his concerns for his wife's mental state; he thought that there was something seriously wrong because she hadn't shown any emotion, good or bad. Sean and Sarah stood close to their father in the cemetery, while Jean stayed close to Maura, who looked so alone standing there beside their graves.

The scream, when it came took everyone by surprise; it sounded like an animal in pain, Maura had began to wail as the caskets were lowered in to the ground, and no one could help to ease her pain, she was totally alone. The priest rushed through the rest of the funeral rite; even he didn't know what to say to Maura to help her through this tragic time. Stephen had organised a meal in O'Donaghue's Hotel, for the family and chief mourners, and anyone else who wanted to join them. Maura wanted to go straight home, but as this was a way to thank people who'd travelled long distances, she knew she had to be there; Stephen had done the right thing, she'd never have thought of it.

'Home Comforts' remained closed for a further two days after the interments, but opened on the Thursday at Maura's request; the girls in the office had been hoping to have the rest of the week off, Maura's request put paid to that. No one actually expected Maura to turn up at the office; they were discussing the inheritance that she would come into, when Maura walked through the door. Luckily, Maura hadn't heard any of the contents of that conversation; if she had, they'd be looking for new jobs. There was plenty of work to catch up on, so there was no excuse for anybody to be standing around gossiping; which was what they'd been doing when Maura walked in, she wasn't stupid, she knew they'd been talking about her, she just didn't know what had been said. For a couple of hours Maura went through some of the paperwork, before deciding to give Larry a call at the bank, just to tell him the awful thing that had happened to her. Larry was still having his calls screened, but Maura told his secretary that her parents had died and that he'd want to know; the secretary sympathised with her, and said she'd make sure to pass this information on to her boss. Maura thought that she was probably lying, but she realised that she didn't care; Larry wasn't important to her any more, nothing was important now. Twenty minutes later Larry returned her call, he was truly sorry to hear her sad news; he never knew them but he could imagine what Maura was going through. Maura thanked him for his kind words of sympathy and was about to say goodbye when Larry asked her if she would like to meet up for a drink some time, if she needed to talk he was there. He must have forgotten about the solicitor's letter, but Maura hadn't; she didn't even know why she'd rang him, she didn't need to talk to him. He meant nothing to her, she felt nothing for anyone at the moment; not even her family. She prayed that no one said that time would heal, or that each day it would get easier; she didn't need clichés, she needed her mother and father, but she wasn't going to get that, she'd never see them again. The finality of it was like a physical blow; she shrank down in to the chair and wept for a long time. The girls in the outer office could hear her sobs, but thought it best not to disturb her, she was probably better to let it all out; they considered ringing Stephen but thought better of it. Maura was crying for herself as much as for her parents, she was angry with them for leaving her, they should have driven more carefully, they knew she'd be waiting for them. She wouldn't have to buy any more pastries now, she wondered what had happened to the last lot she'd bought; Jean had probably thrown them out, what a waste she thought. The day was going from bad to worse for Maura, she was sorry that she'd gone into work in the first place; Larry must have felt sorry for her and that was why he'd rang her back, but she couldn't think about him at the moment. Stephen rang her to see if she'd be home early, but the girls told him that she'd already left, more than half an hour ago. Maura was in the cemetery, she'd gone there to talk to her parents; she wanted to give out to them for not being more careful, but realised it wasn't their fault. This was something that no one had wanted to happen; it was an accident plain and simple. Before Maura left the graveyard she looked across at a young couple who were placing flowers on a tiny grave, moving towards them she saw that the woman was crying. They were standing beside their baby daughter's grave; Maura knew then that she wasn't the only person hurting. Death didn't care what age a person was, it didn't discriminate on the grounds of age; Maura had to come to terms with losing her parents. When she arrived home her family were there waiting for her, Sarah had been scared in case anything had happened to her; Stephen and Sean were relieved to see her, but didn't let on how worried they'd been. Maura was pleased with the welcome she got, she knew now that she should have phoned to let them know she was all right; and she was all right, or at least she would be one day.

Life wasn't going to stand still just because she was grieving, she hadn't thought about her children during this period, they'd lost their grandparents but Maura hadn't given them a moments thought; not much of a mother, she thought. She had relied too much on Jean, not just since her parents had died, but for several years, to take care of her children. Maura wondered when she'd first started leaving Jean to take care of things, her business shouldn't have taken precedence over her family; but it had, and this realisation made Maura sad. As she had proved herself capable of running a successful business, she realised that she didn't have to do it any more. Her main objective, when starting the company, was to prove she could do it and to make her parents proud of her; they always were proud of her, she just didn't know it. Everything they had owned was now hers, the home in Waterford, all the money in their bank accounts; even Stephen's company, it all belonged to her now. One of the first things that Maura was going to do was to pay a visit to her solicitor, she wanted to make sure that her children's inheritance was in order; at the thought of a solicitor Larry's name came to mind. She would ring him to thank him for his concern, but she wouldn't meet him; her parents would have been disappointed in her if they'd known she was seeing a married man, and she didn't want to disappoint them. It might be the right time to cut Jean's hours, she'd still pay her the same wage, but she'd suggest that she go back to three days a week instead of five, and Maura could be at home for the other two days. Jean could hardly object to Maura spending more time with her own children, she might even be glad of the time off, she wasn't getting any younger. Maura would sound her out in a few weeks time, when she'd things organised at work; she was considering selling 'Home Comforts', it had lost its appeal for her, she'd taken it as far as she could. Maybe her designers would put in an offer for the company, she could give them first refusal; but she was getting ahead of herself, she shouldn't make any decisions for a while, but she could think about it. Stephen wouldn't mind what she did, poor old Stephen, he'd been so good; he'd done more than his share at her parents wake and afterwards at the burial, Maura would never have thought to organise a meal for the mourners. Maura couldn't remember if she'd even thanked him for all he'd done, she knew Stephen wouldn't want thanking, he just did what he thought was right.

Chapter 9

Maura's acceptance of her parents' death had happened quite suddenly, though everyone concerned was glad that she'd finally acknowledged it, especially her children who needed her to be there for them. The summer holidays loomed, and the promised trip to Egypt was arranged for the end of August; Stephen was staying at home, he didn't like the hot weather that they could expect in the North African country. Sean wasn't too keen on being away for three weeks, his girlfriend wasn't too happy either but Maura wouldn't hear of him stopping at home, his father wouldn't exactly be able to keep an eye on him. Maura had put off the decision of whether to sell the interior design company, or whether to appoint a manager to run it for her. Jean's hours were trimmed down which suited both her and Maura; Jean had been thinking of finishing altogether, but this new arrangement suited her better. Sarah's tenth birthday was a quiet affair, which was what she had wanted, but the absence of her grandparents had a sombre effect on the festivities. The weather was the only saving grace, it was warm enough for them to eat out in the garden and the sound of the birds singing had an uplifting side to it.

The summer holidays always came and went too quickly, their three weeks in Egypt flew by; they spent the first week cruising down the river Nile, and the other two weeks at a resort on the Red Sea Coast. El Gouna was a newly built resort with everything available on site; the water sports included scuba diving, water skiing and for the more experienced the deep sea diving which was supposed to be spectacular. Sean and Sarah spent a lot of time in the lagoon, which was part of the Red Sea and which was adjacent to the hotel complex. Maura relaxed on one of the comfortable loungers that surrounded the lagoon, ensuring that her offspring were being supervised in the water, their safety was her prime concern. Their nights were spent dining in the luxury hotel dining room, or in the nearby town of Hurghada, to which they travelled to on the bus provided by the hotel. Maura purchased some small mementoes to bring back for the girls in the office, for her three favourite designers, Maura was able to pick up some beautiful Egyptian cotton; she knew that Ciara in particular would love this. The holiday had done them good, they had managed to laugh for the first time since the funeral; they even reminisced about some of the holidays they'd spent in Waterford. Maura was pleased that the children had such good memories of her parents, and she hoped that they were listening to this wherever they where. When it came to the end of their holiday they each agreed that it had been the best holiday that they'd ever had and they'd definitely come back; their one regret was that they hadn't taken a trip to Cairo to visit the pyramids, still this gave them an excuse to come back next year.

Maura had come to a decision about her company, 'Home Comforts', she was going to keep it on for the next year but after that she was going to sell it; she would definitely be giving her designers first refusal. Maura would speak to all her staff when she went back to work, the following week. This would give anyone who was interested, time to get their finances organised, it would also ensure that when the time came Maura would be able to hand over the company without too much hassle. In that way the company wouldn't suffer either and this was important to Maura, it had been her baby for the last few years; looking back now it was the best thing she'd ever done. Now the decision to sell the company was made, Maura was quite happy to go back home; she had other ideas for new ventures, and life no longer looked so bleak.

Stephen was at the airport to meet them, he'd missed them and he was sorry that he hadn't gone with them. Even Maura seemed pleased to see him, and his children seemed more grown up even though it had only been three weeks that they'd been away. Jean had been at the house when he'd left for the airport, she was cooking a special dinner for them; to welcome them home, she'd kept Stephen supplied with hot dinners while the rest of the family were on holiday. Stephen was well able to cook his own dinners but he liked being fussed over, and Jean wanted to feel useful, so it suited them both. Maura jokingly told her husband that he could pay her wages from now on, Stephen's mouth dropped, he could do without any more expenses; business was rather slow at the moment. The real problem was that he wasn't putting any effort into it right now, and if something didn't change soon, he'd have no business left. Maura had trusted her husband to run the business without her constantly looking over his shoulder, and so she had no idea how bad the situation was; but Stephen knew that he'd have to tell her, and soon.

After the heat of Egypt, the cool weather in Dublin was a relief; cool being 20 degrees centigrade. Sarah chatted non-stop about their holiday; she named nearly all the places they'd visited from Luxor down to Aswan. They'd visited the great temple of the God Horus, at Edfu; they went to the temple of Philae near Aswan where they enjoyed the magnificent sound and light show. Sarah raced on, telling her father about riding camels in the Sahara desert and visiting a Nubian village that had stone beds. Maura had to tell her daughter to slow down and keep some of her stories for later; she was in danger of trying to cram three weeks worth of adventure into an hour. Stephen agreed, he'd much prefer to hear the full story and not just the highlights; he wanted all the details and he wanted to see their videos, when they got home. Stephen told Sarah that he'd expect a running commentary, with nothing left out; this seemed to have the desired effect, and it appeased her. When Sarah was silent, Sean told his father that he should have come with them, as he'd been outnumbered by the women; and they were mostly old biddies as far as he was concerned. Stephen was pleased that the children had missed him, and that they would have liked it if he'd gone with them. Maura, Stephen noted hadn't commented one way or the other, but she had looked happy to see him at the airport; but maybe that was because he'd be driving them home, not to mention he'd be pushing the luggage trolley for them.

The rest of the drive home was in relative silence; Sarah had stopped talking and the others followed suit. Stephen guessed that they must be shattered after their five-hour flight, not to mention the journey to the airport in Luxor; he knew they'd had a very early start, they had to be exhausted. After travelling for eight or nine hours, a decent meal, a shower and then a few hours sleep was the order of the day. They would have plenty of time to catch up later, with all the news etc.

Stephen couldn't stop smiling to himself, he was so glad that they were home. Maura was quiet, she was obviously tired but Stephen sensed that there was something else on her mind, he'd have to wait till she was ready to tell him; you couldn't rush Maura. At last they pulled into their driveway, and Jean opened the front door even before Stephen had switched off the engine; Sean and Sarah were delighted that she was there to meet them. Maura too was pleased that she was there, they could catch up on any gossip that was going round; Stephen never seemed to hear any. Jean had cooked a roast chicken and plenty of fresh vegetables, she said that someone had told her that they didn't have many vegetables in Egypt; Maura didn't like to correct her. The smell of home cooking made their mouths water and the tiredness was forgotten for the time being, while they tucked in to the delicious dinner that was waiting for them. After dinner Stephen took their bags up to their rooms and left them to unpack in peace, Maura didn't bother unpacking; she just wanted a quick shower before heading to bed. The two children unpacked their souvenirs and the presents they'd brought back for some of their school friends; they hadn't forgotten their father, they'd bought him several pyramids of varying sizes and colours. It wasn't long before the children too went to bed, Sean insisted on phoning his girlfriend first, unfortunately she wasn't at home; he'd have to wait till later to get hold of her. The house was once again quiet, Stephen debated whether he should talk to his wife, that evening, about the state of the business; but he wisely decided that it would be better to leave it for a few days, he'd let her get settled back in. They all slept for about three hours and came downstairs still in their night attire; they were only planning on staying up for a short while. Sean and Sarah presented Stephen with the selection of alabaster paperweights in the shape of pyramids, which they claimed were supposed to be lucky; they weren't sure why, they just were. Stephen didn't care what they were meant to be, to him they were priceless; he knew that they had been bought with love, he'd cherish them always. Maura had bought him some new bath sheets for his en suite, they were made from the best Egyptian cotton; she planned changing the tiles in his bathroom, the old ones had been there since they'd bought the house, at least eighteen years ago. Maura couldn't believe how long they'd been married, where had the years gone? She felt sad that she and Stephen had drifted apart so early on in their marriage. Her husband was at a disadvantage to start with, she was still in love with Tomas, when she got together with Stephen; he didn't stand a chance. When Sean and Sarah had gone to bed, Maura sat down with Stephen to tell him what she had decided with regards to 'Home Comforts'. Though Stephen was surprised he thought that Maura knew what she was doing; she knew the market and she knew when to go. He felt sure that she would be able to sort out his problems, once he told her the situation; he had to admit, and not for the first time, that Maura was the one with the brains and not him. In a way, once he acknowledged this he didn't feel so bad, and he hoped that Maura would see it this way too.

Maura was amazed that her husband had been so supportive when she told him of her decision to sell her interior design company, in a year's time, she thought he'd complain that he'd lose business from 'Home Comforts'; which may or may not happen. Once Maura sold up, she would no longer have any influence as to what painting and decorating company they'd use. Surely by now though, Stephen could manage with out the extra work he got from 'Home Comforts', at least he should be able to; his decorating firm was on the go a long time now, it was well established. Little did Maura know that Stephen's firm was in severe trouble, due entirely to his incompetence and lack of foresight; and laziness had a big part in it. There was a lot of work to be done if his business were to survive, and the sooner he told Maura the better; at least he should have the courage to admit his mistakes, and give his wife a fighting chance to pull the business back from the brink of bankruptcy. Maura was going to have a tough few months ahead; she didn't know it yet though.

Maura's first week back at work passed very quickly, there hadn't been any problems while she was on holiday; the company was running smoothly, with work coming in all the time. So far Maura kept the news to herself about selling her company, she wanted to go through the books and make sure that everything was in order. She had made an appointment for the following week, to see her accountant and her solicitor; then she would decide when to let her staff know of her intentions to sell.

Sean was starting his Junior Cert. year, while Sarah was starting in secondary school; both were looking forward to seeing their friends after the summer holidays. During the second week back at work, Sinead told Maura that she needed to have a word with her; in private. This sounded a bit ominous to Maura who was hoping that Sinead wasn't going to be giving in her notice. The designer was a major asset to 'Home Comforts'; and besides Maura didn't like to think that her employees weren't happy working for her. Maura said that they could have lunch together in the nearby pizza hut; she knew that Sinead loved pizzas and hopefully this would put her at her ease. Lunchtime came around quickly and the two women headed out to lunch, none of the other staff thought anything odd about this. Sinead was dreading what she was about to tell Maura, and she felt uncomfortable; she'd drawn the short straw at work, as both Holly and Ciara knew what was going on. They ordered their lunch and a glass of wine each before Maura asked Sinead what was troubling her. Sinead explained that she'd been delegated the job of telling Maura about the rumours circulating about Stephen's business. Maura hadn't a clue what she was talking about; she wanted to know what rumours were going around about her husband's business. She had every right to know. Sinead said that they'd all heard the same rumours that the business was on the verge of bankruptcy, they hoped it wasn't true but this knowledge seemed to be widespread now. The girls didn't want Maura to hear this information from outside the office; they thought that if she hadn't heard it from Stephen by now then they felt it their duty to tell her.

Maura was speechless, she couldn't believe what she was hearing; and if it was true, then she was going to kill Stephen. Maura asked Sinead if it was common knowledge among the office staff about Stephen's problems. As far as Sinead knew, it wasn't, at least her and the other designers hadn't heard any gossip from them. Thank God thought Maura, at least she wouldn't have to endure any sympathetic looks from them or talking behind her back; the office staff weren't as loyal to her as her designers. Maura told Sinead of her fears that she had been about to give in her notice, and of her relief that this wasn't the case; she asked Sinead to ask the others to keep this information to themselves. Maura was very disappointed in Stephen, he must realise that she was going to find out sooner or later; and as far as she was concerned it should have been sooner rather than later. She knew he'd been behaving strangely recently, but this was the last thing that she'd expected to hear. Not only was he letting her down he was also letting her parents down; Maura was going to have to save the business one way or another. It might now be necessary to sell her company sooner than she had planned to, not because she needed the money but rather to concentrate on Stephen's company. Her parents' death had left her a very wealthy woman, but this wasn't the point; it was a matter of principle that the company did well; or else Maura felt they were letting her parents down. Maura had an almost overwhelming urge to phone Larry, for some reason whenever she got upset, her thoughts turned to her ex. Maura thought better of phoning Larry, that relationship was better left in the past, she had more pressing things on her mind.

Of late Stephen had gone up in Maura's estimation, and for this to happen with the business, it was coming at a very inopportune time; he was now down at the bottom of the heap. If Maura had despised him in the past, this was nothing to how she felt right now; Stephen had better have some good excuses, and hopefully the rumours were just that; rumours. Leaving the office early, Maura went straight home; she wanted to check over Stephen's accounts, before accusing him without proof of any wrongdoing. When she arrived home she went straight to their office off the kitchen, she didn't stop to speak to Jean, except to say hello. While Maura was waiting for the computer to boot up, she wondered if Jean was aware of any problems in the decorating company, she'd talk to her later. Thank goodness for broadband Maura didn't have long to wait to pull up the relevant documents, it took a little longer to wade through Stephen's system; and by the time she'd finished she was spitting fire. How could he be so stupid as to let things get in to such a state, and she knew that this hadn't just happened overnight; things had been bad for a long time, and she should have kept a closer watch on his business. Maura's head began to throb; she was shocked that her husband was so dim-witted as to think she wouldn't find out about the state of affairs the company was in. Sometimes Maura felt so alone in her marriage and she wondered, not for the first time, why she didn't kick her husband's sorry arse out on the street, and let him fend for himself. Why did they always seem to take one step forward and two steps back, and why did she keep making allowances for him? After this, Maura was going to take over managing the company, Stephen would have no say in it, he'd continue as the painter and decorator, but that was as far as his contribution would go. Jean was in the kitchen when Maura came out of the office; her demeanour confirmed the humour she was in. The two ladies sat down at the kitchen table to have a cup of coffee and for Maura to quiz Jean about Stephen's lack of business acumen; with Maura hoping that Jean knew nothing of his disastrous dealings. Jean did have an inkling, she said, that Stephen was experiencing some financial difficulties; but at the end of the day she didn't think it was up to her to mention it. Maura gritted her teeth in rage; she had expected a different response from her housekeeper, who was more a confidante than employee. This would certainly change the way Maura thought of her in future; if indeed she had a future with them. By now Maura was feeling hurt that she seemed to be the last to know that there were any problems in the firm that her parents had set up for her useless husband. There were going to be ructions when Stephen got home from work; the word work stuck in Maura's throat, and she wondered what he actually did every day, it sure as hell wasn't what Maura's idea of work was. It was no wonder his weight had piled on again, the lazy good for nothing; Maura was running out of words to describe her husband, even if it was only in her head, she had no intention of telling Jean what she thought of her husband. She'd always been good to her; she couldn't understand how she could now turn around and say that she didn't think it was her place to tell Maura what was happening. The saying, you live and learn sprang to mind, and Maura thought back to when she first gave Jean a job; even back then she paid her over the going rate. The more Maura thought about Jean the more annoyed she became, even Maura's parents had been good to her; they'd left her five thousand euro in their will. Maura almost spat this fact out at Jean, but decided not to show her hand just yet, she wanted to think things through before she acted. Jean looked a little on edge, possibly because she realised that she hadn't been very fair to Maura; but probably because she knew first hand how vindictive her employer could be. Maura was not a person to be crossed and until now Jean never thought that she had done. When Maura finished drinking her coffee, she made some small talk with Jean; she wasn't prepared to give Jean any idea of how she was feeling. Sending Jean home early wasn't an option either, as this would alert the housekeeper to the fact that she was in very bad form; there was time enough for that. Looking at her watch, Maura knew that Stephen would be home in a couple of hours, and she had things to do before then. Maura left Jean to get on with cooking the dinner, while she went back to the office and the accounts; her eyes welled up with tears, and she wanted to be alone to shed them. Maura cried for herself and her family, she didn't want to have to make decisions that would affect them; so soon after the death of her parents, she didn't need this now. She went back out to the kitchen, and thankfully Jean was somewhere else in the house, Maura needed a large brandy; and she didn't want Jean to see her getting it. Maura now considered her a turncoat, but why Jean should feel any loyalty to Stephen was something she couldn't understand; Stephen wasn't the one who paid her wages. However, that wasn't too important; some women couldn't help themselves when a weak man was involved. Drinking the brandy, while sitting in front of the computer gave Maura time to consider all her options; she definitely wasn't going to be hasty, there was more than one way to skin a cat, as the saying goes. Maura always considered the saying, marry in haste repent at leisure, and this was more than apt in her and Stephen's case. The brandy was going down well and she no longer wanted to cry, she was calm and quite rational in her thoughts; she knew exactly what she was going to do. She also knew what she was going to say to her husband once Jean had gone home; and she was going to wait till her children had gone up to their rooms to do their homework, before confronting him.

Maura switched off the computer before going up to her bedroom, she was in need of a quick shower before the children got home from school, they always managed to cheer her up; no matter how rotten her day had been. She had just finished dressing when she heard her children being dropped off; Maura took it in turns to drive her children and a neighbour's child to school, which worked out well for both families. Going downstairs, Maura heard the usual banter between her son and daughter taking place, and once again she felt a great sense of pride in them. They were pleased to see that their mother was home before them, but wondered if there was a particular reason for this; Maura reassured them that she just wanted to spend the extra time with them. They at least didn't need to be worried about adult problems; Maura tried to protect them as much as possible from unnecessary fears. Sarah in particular, was a little worrier and still cried sometimes over her grandparents' deaths; she'd been close to them, even though she was very young when they'd moved to Waterford. Sarah had talked to them almost every night on the phone and she loved to spend the holidays with them, they treated her with respect and listened to her worries; she missed them so much. Maura's mother had always kept her up to date on any concerns that the children might have, she felt that her daughter was entitled to know if her children had any problems. Of course Maura kept anything she was told to herself, she wouldn't betray her parent's confidence; and this is how it should be. It was a pity that more people, namely Jean, didn't see things the same way as she did. It was almost time for Jean to go home, and Maura didn't think it would come soon enough; she wanted her gone before Stephen arrived home. Maura didn't want Jean to have a chance to alert her husband to the fact that she knew about the business being in trouble. That was her privilege. At last Jean collected her bag and put on her shoes in readiness for going home; Maura wished her a safe journey home, as she always did, and said she'd see her in two days time, on the Wednesday. Maura was pleased that she'd been able to keep her cool with her housekeeper; she hoped she'd be able to do the same with her husband.

Chapter 10

While Maura waited for Stephen to put in an appearance, she talked to Sean about his expectations in Junior Cert. year; he'd mentioned that he'd like to find out what subjects he'd need if he was to go on to study architecture at university. Maura was pleased that he had aspirations to go to university after leaving school, and he seemed to be happy enough since this term had started. Sarah was listening to her big brother talking about university and she was proud of him. Suddenly she realised that if he went away, she'd be on her own with just her parents for company; no way could she stay there without her big brother, she'd miss him too much. Just then Maura heard Stephen's key turn in the door, he was a little later than usual and she hoped that he hadn't ran into Jean; who was quite likely to have waited around outside to talk to him. As soon as he walked in to the kitchen, Maura knew she was right; Jean had warned him, she knew it by the look on his face; she wasn't going to say anything to him until the children were upstairs doing their homework. Stephen made some pathetic small talk, before telling Maura that he had something important to tell her, when the children were in bed later. Maura wasn't going to let him dictate to her as to when they'd talk, she would choose the time; not Stephen. Smiling across the table at Stephen,

Maura kept her voice calm when she said that they'd have plenty of time to talk after dinner; which was ready to be served up. Stephen visibly relaxed, thinking that Jean had probably exaggerated Maura's frame of mind, she seemed pretty unruffled to him. Maura knew that Stephen had been expecting her to fly off the handle, the minute he walked through the door; and she was happy to let him think what ever he liked. Dinner was a noisy affair, with everyone talking at once; Maura kept up the conversation while she loaded the dishwasher, and the children headed upstairs to do their homework.

Maura asked Stephen to pour them a drink, while she finished tidying up in the kitchen; she told Stephen that she'd had a bitch of a day and needed to unwind, 'anything for you honey bun,' said Stephen getting the brandy out. He didn't see his wife cringe at this term of endearment; he didn't really know his wife at all, even though they'd been married for more years than he could remember.

Maura pottered around in the kitchen, giving her husband time to settle in his favourite chair with his drink in hand and a silly grin on his face; instinctively she knew he'd have a stupid grin on his face, and she was right. Maura had been up to check on her children, they were in their own rooms, and seemed to be getting on with their homework without the need for supervision. She didn't want to disturb them so she said she'd be up again before they got ready for bed, this was their usual routine on a school night. Going down to the sitting room, Maura could feel her heart beating faster, due in part to what she was going to say to her husband; and partly due to the fact that Jean had been disloyal to her again. She sat down wearily on the sofa, and she took a large mouthful of her drink and tried to steady herself before she talked to Stephen.

'Well honey bun,' she said sarcastically, 'and what have you been up to lately?' Maura didn't wait for his reply, instead she went on to tell him exactly what he'd been up to, or more importantly; what he hadn't been up to, which was work as she pointed out.

'What have you been doing each day when you leave the house? Because it sure as hell wasn't work,' she shouted. Maura lowered her voice, she didn't want the children to come down, at least not till she'd finished with their father. She started again, not wanting to give him a chance to wheedle out of it this time, because this wasn't the first time that he'd made a mess of the business. So many times in the past she told him to keep receipts for everything, their accountant couldn't do his job properly without valid receipts; and so many times he'd underpriced jobs, and ended up losing money on them. Maura told Stephen she'd had enough of his idiocy, he couldn't be trusted running the business any more; he was running it in to the ground, and Maura wasn't going to let that happen. Stephen held his head in his hands and cried softly.

'You big lummox, what the hell are you crying for? It's not as if it'll cost you anything to sort this out,' said Maura, again trying to control her voice.

Stephen stopped snivelling and apologised over and over for letting things slide again. He didn't realise how bad things were until one of the lads working for him told him that he'd heard that people were laughing at his boss for undercharging for jobs. Stephen was a pitiful sight, though Maura was prepared to let it go this time, she couldn't keep bailing him out; he was a liability, and he wasn't any use to the business in a managerial capacity. Maura told him that she'd be taking over all the day to day running of the firm, and if he chose, he could stay on as an employee of hers. She made it quite clear that he could take it or leave it, this wasn't up for discussion; and Stephen knew she meant it this time. All in all he thought he'd got off lightly, Maura could have said a lot more, and a lot worse. There was one other thing that Maura had to tell him, and that was that, if he didn't pull his finger out and work like a Trojan then, he'd be out of a job and out of his home; he was on his last chance. Stephen went down on his knees and promised that he wouldn't let her down; he would do whatever she said. His pleading only served to infuriate her more and she told him to get out of her sight, which he promptly did; he took his drink with him and went to the kitchen, again he knew he'd got off lightly. Maura was sick of these confrontations and she knew she had no alternative but to let Jean go, she wouldn't have her in her employment any more. It would probably cost her a month's wages, but she just wasn't prepared to have someone working for her if she couldn't trust them, and that was all there was to it. She was keeping that little snippet of news to herself, she couldn't tell Stephen, as she didn't trust him not to warn Jean in advance. Maura went in to the kitchen to get herself another drink; Stephen was drinking a can of Guinness and watching a football match on the television. He hadn't heard his wife coming in, and when he did see her he didn't know if he should say anything, he was afraid he'd say the wrong thing so he said nothing. Maura would have bitten his head off if he had said anything, right now she didn't want to listen to anything he might have to say; she was tired, it had been a bitch of a day. The children would be finished their homework by now, so Maura left her drink in the sitting room and went upstairs to check on them; and to find out if they'd heard her and Stephen. They each had music on so Maura knew they wouldn't have heard them, and Maura had been careful to keep her voice low; they had finished their homework and were ready for bed. Wishing them good night, Maura said she'd have a look over their homework in the morning; she then went back down stairs. It was hard for her to relax, but the brandy did help a little, and when she heard her husband go upstairs to bed she had a third drink; this was more than she'd normally have at home. Maura was a social drinker, and she didn't think it was a good idea to drink at home on a regular basis. Life wasn't being very fair to her at the moment, but at least she had her children; they made up for the bad times. Maura was glad that her children didn't take after their father; she thought that would be a hard cross to bear if they did. Maura felt a little tipsy when she went up to bed, this would help her to sleep she thought; or at least she hoped it would. The drink didn't have the desired effect, and she did a lot of tossing and turning, all the time going over the conversation she was going to have with Jean, in her mind. The alarm went off too early, Maura thought she had probably had just a few hours sleep; she cursed her no good husband for making her need the third drink last night. The children were up and showered by the time Maura got down stairs, she got the porridge going and made some fresh coffee for herself. Stephen was moving around in his bedroom and he stayed there until he heard Maura going back to her room to take her shower, he couldn't face another confrontation so early in the morning. If he was quick enough he could grab some breakfast and still be out of the house before she came down again; he might be more ready to face her in the evening, she might have cooled down a bit by then, though he didn't necessarily believe that.

Sometimes he wished that he could stand up to her, but in this instance, he knew that Maura had every right to be mad at him; it was going to be a rough few weeks ahead. Maura would calm down once she'd got the business back running smoothly, and he had to admit that she was better at managing a business than he was. He would be getting along well for a while, and then somehow he'd get side tracked; and he'd lose sight of what he should be doing. Maybe some day he'd get it right, and then Maura might have more respect for him; she'd treat him better then. Stephen had almost convinced himself that it was his wife's fault that the business was in trouble, until he remembered that she had given him a free hand to run it as he saw fit. His only hope was to keep his head down and keep out of Maura's way for the time being; for now his biggest problem was to sneak out of the house without her seeing him; which he did in the nick of time.

Maura's head was starting to throb, and she wasn't sure if it was from the drink or the tension between Stephen and her. She had heard him leaving, he was probably avoiding her, and she was glad that she didn't have to see him this morning. The children's lift would be here at any minute, and then Maura would do the small amount of housework that needed to be done; she had a good few phone calls to make but it was still too early to make these yet. After the children left, Maura realised she hadn't checked their homework; she cursed Stephen, this was because of him that she was in a state. Men, she thought, life would be easier without them; or at least without her one. Maura had an appointment at 11a.m. with their accountant and one in the afternoon with their solicitor. She had briefed both on the reason for wanting to see them; and hoped that they'd be able to come up with some suggestions to rescue the business. Maura wasn't stupid enough to plough more money into a company that didn't stand a chance of succeeding; regardless of the fact that her parents had started this company. Her father always said that there was no room for sentiment in business, and Maura always tried to follow his advice; he was a self-made millionaire, so he knew what he was talking about. Just thinking about her father made her determined to sort out the mess that her husband had got the business in to. She did make a promise to herself that she wouldn't let Stephen get his hands on the reins again, he'd had more than enough chances in the past; and he'd failed miserably each time. When Maura had come out from her meetings, she felt that she'd been through the wringer; she was going to have to pump a lot of capital into the business in order to save it. Her accountant said it had been a good business in the past and he said he thought it was worth hanging on to it. Maura had a few days to make up her mind; she needed time to think about it before coming to a decision.

Sometimes Maura felt that she couldn't go on being married to a man who just seemed to make her life miserable; in the past she thought the children would suffer if they became a one-parent family. Now, Maura thought that they'd probably be better off with just her, their father never contributed much to their upbringing. This week was going to be a major decision making one and not least of all because Maura was tired of her husband's failings. A big decision that Maura had to make was, if she pulled the plug on Stephen's business, then where did that leave him? Effectively, he would be out of a job. The day after visiting her accountant and solicitor, Maura rang her receptionist in 'Home Comforts' to let them know that she would be working from home that day;

she was in reality awaiting Jean's arrival, this was going to be her day of dismissal. Maura wouldn't tolerate disloyalty, not from Jean or anyone else. As yet Stephen knew nothing of her plans; Maura had already been on to the agency from which she'd employed Jean, over sixteen years ago. She had told the agency that she wanted someone who would be totally reliable, loyal and trustworthy, someone who would appreciate a good employer. Maura always paid top wages to her staff, this usually ensured that she got the best; and up until now she couldn't fault Jean, she'd been indispensable. The new cleaner/housekeeper would only be required on a part-time basis, but she would be required to be there three afternoons per week, from 12p.m. to 5p.m. On an odd occasion she might be asked to either come in earlier or stay later; and on an even odder occasion, she might be needed to work an extra day once in a while.

The agency assured Maura that they would be able to supply her with the perfect employee, and she would be sent to her house that afternoon for an interview; they were positive that she was the ideal person to fill the position available. Jean was just about to turn her key in the front door when Maura opened it, Jean had got a fright, she didn't expect anyone to be at home; and usually at this time of the day the house was empty. Maura had just two words to say to Jean and they were, 'You're Fired'.

Jean stared at Maura to see if this was a joke, but she soon realised that it wasn't; she tried to explain her actions of two days ago, but Maura didn't want to hear her excuses. Maura handed Jean an envelope containing three months' wages, in lieu of notice and asked for her door key back. Jean pleaded with her to listen to her reasons about why she'd kept quiet about Stephen's troubles with the business, and why she'd warned him that Maura knew about it; Maura told her to tell it to someone who cared. With that ringing in her ears Jean handed the key back to Maura, who then closed the door without uttering another word. Jean had never felt so humiliated in her whole life, she couldn't believe that Maura would treat her like that; she had worked hard all her life, and didn't expect to be dismissed in this fashion. Jean rang Stephen as soon as she got home, but his mobile was engaged and she didn't want to leave a message; she'd try his phone again later. Maura had felt a great satisfaction when she closed the door on Jean, she was almost certain that she'd be on the phone to Stephen before the day was over. Maura knew that Jean was old fashioned, but why she felt she had a duty to Stephen was a mystery; and some day she intended to find out.

Maura had a few jobs to do at home, and she spent the next two hours on the computer going over a business plan to save the company that Stephen seemed intent on ruining. Once her mind was made up, Maura rang her accountant and told him of her decision; he could now set the wheels in motion. She made a second call to her solicitor, also informing him of her intentions; she wouldn't be ringing her husband. He'd have to wait until the evening before she'd let him know her decision on the business, and she hoped that he would be sweating about it. Stephen was in a bit of a sweat, Jean had rung him to tell him that his wife had fired her; she was in a dreadful state over it. Stephen knew that he was partly responsible for this situation, but he didn't know what he could do to change Maura's mind, besides which he couldn't imagine the two women ever getting on again. He told Jean that he'd try to talk to his wife that evening, but he wasn't promising anything, he knew that Maura wasn't going to listen to anything that he had to say. He worried that the children would be very upset when they realised that they wouldn't be seeing Jean any more, and he didn't know what his wife was going to tell them. Stephen had worked hard that day, he really wanted to make amends for his past mistakes, and he knew it would take a miracle for Maura to forgive him, but he had to try. The woman that was sent over from the agency, for the job interview; made a good impression on Maura; and she decided to give her a trial period, after which she'd either keep her on or she'd give her her marching orders. Niamh was in her early thirties, and she had good references from a previous employer, she had left her previous position because the family were moving to America; Niamh wanted to remain in Ireland, she had family here. Maura liked her straight away, she was down to earth and very flexible with her hours; she was available to work whatever hours her future employer wanted. This was exactly what Maura wanted to hear, she just hoped that her children took to Niamh, and that they didn't get too upset when they learned that Jean wouldn't be around any more. Children were adaptable, at least that's what their mother hoped, and she would be spending more time at home in the near future.

Both Sean and Sarah wanted to know where Jean was when they came in from school, Maura sat them down and told them that Jean was getting a little too old to keep house for them; they were upset but accepted this explanation. Sarah said that she would visit Jean and that she could always phone her at the weekends. Maura said nothing in reply to this, she knew her daughter would be busy with other things and she'd soon forget about ringing Jean. Sean was very quiet when he heard the news, he wasn't as trusting as his sister; and he knew when his mother wasn't telling the full truth, he'd ask his father later. Maura took a chicken curry from the freezer and put it in the microwave to thaw, she checked to make sure that she had enough rice, and then she set the table for dinner. Stephen wouldn't be home for another hour and a half, and during this time Maura talked to Sinead, she suggested they go out with the other girls some night soon, it had been too long since they'd hit the town. Sinead said she was up for it, and she'd only been saying the same thing to the others last week; they too would be up for it. After her phone calls Maura went back to the kitchen to prepare their dinner, she overheard Sean telling Sarah that he thought their mother wasn't telling the truth about why Jean had left. Maura pretended that she hadn't heard him, there was no need to make a big deal out of it, her son was smart, and he wouldn't pursue it. Sarah asked who would be there in the house when they came home from school, she didn't want to come home to an empty house on the days when Maura was at work. Maura said that there was a new housekeeper starting next week, but she was going to call over to meet them tomorrow evening. She told them about Niamh, and said that she seemed like a really nice woman; Maura told them that if they didn't get on with her then she wouldn't keep her on, this was a trial period only. Maura said that maybe Niamh might not like them, and she might not want to look after them; she suggested that they all give Niamh a fair go.

Stephen came home at 6p.m., slightly earlier than he was expected, he said that he'd finished the job in record time and that every thing was set for the next day; he looked across at Maura pleadingly. He kept up a non-stop account of all the work he'd done that day, in the hope of impressing his wife, but he was wasting his time; too little too late thought Maura. Her husband was going to have to work his butt off for the rest of his working life if he wanted to impress her. When they were almost finished their dinner, Stephen mentioned his phone call from Jean; Maura stopped him from saying what the phone call was about, she took over the conversation and told him the same version she'd given to the children. For once her husband caught on to what she was trying to tell him, he knew better than to contradict her, and he was sure that she would tell him her reasons for getting rid of Jean; he was pretty sure that he already knew the reason. Sure enough, once the children had gone upstairs to do their homework, Maura let fly at him, she had a very sharp tongue when she was angry. She asked him why he was so stupid as to almost tell the children the real reason that Jean was no longer welcome. Did he really want them to know what a mess he'd made of the business? Maura didn't think that he wanted to tell them how lazy he'd been, or how incompetent or how useless he was; but she said that he could go ahead and tell them the truth if that's what he wanted. Stephen knew that Maura was right, he didn't want his children to know any of that, he was glad that Maura hadn't given him a chance to open his big mouth about Jean. Once again Maura had saved his bacon, he wondered if he'd ever get things right; God knows he hadn't done up till now, he hoped that she'd give him another chance. As yet Maura hadn't told him what was happening about the company, and if she was going to save it or not; it was important to her but she wouldn't be sentimental unless it was worth saving.

Stephen couldn't believe he'd let things go wrong again, he obviously wasn't cut out to manage a company, and it was about time he admitted it. He knew he was a good manual worker, when he wasn't under pressure; he just couldn't manage the books and he was hopeless at keeping receipts and things. Maura came in from the kitchen to where Stephen was waiting for her, she didn't beat around the bush, and she told him that she was going to bail the company out of its financial difficulties. She herself was going to take over the running of the company and he was going to work his socks off for the rest of his life; he could take it or leave it, and if he ever let her down again he was out on his ear. Maura mentioned that she was going to sell 'Home Comforts', not because she had to, she had made this decision while she was in Egypt before knowing about the trouble Stephen was in. Maura promised to cut his tongue out if he so much as breathed a word about this before she was ready to tell anyone; Stephen didn't doubt that she wouldn't carry out her threat, and he had no intention of suffering that fate. He swore that he wouldn't tell a soul, and he meant it; he considered himself very lucky to be still living in the same house as his family. Maura was quite sure that her husband could be trusted with the information about selling 'Home Comforts'; he valued his life too much. It had been a long day for Maura but she was pleased with her decisions, and she was pleased that the children hadn't given her any grief over Jean's sudden departure. She went upstairs to spend a little time with them before they went to bed, Sarah still had some homework to do but Sean had finished, and he enjoyed his mother's company, they often had long chats in the evenings. Maura would also spend some time with Sarah, when she'd finished writing her English essay; her daughter was the quieter of her children. Stephen popped his head round the door to say goodnight to the children, he was going to have an early night, and he said he would be making an early start the next day. They all wished each other a goodnight; at least they could still be civil to one another.

Chapter 11

Sean and Sarah got on well with Niamh, and it was obvious from the start that Niamh liked the teenagers; which was a relief to Maura, who was afraid that they'd compare her unfavourably to Jean. Stephen kept his thoughts to himself; he knew Maura didn't want to hear his opinion; even though it was favourable. The trial period for Niamh came and went, and both parties were happy with the working arrangements. At last Maura felt that she could leave some of the day-to-day running of the household to her new housekeeper. Maura had made it very clear to Niamh from the outset, that loyalty was the most important requisite for the position of housekeeper. Niamh was aware of the reason for the departure of the last housekeeper, and she vowed never to be in the same position as her predecessor. She realised from the start that this job was perfect for her, and she knew that she was being paid a fantastic wage; the best that she'd ever been paid, and she didn't want to jeopardise that. Maura was kept extremely busy running the two businesses, but she still managed to spend quality time with her children. Sean had got excellent results in his Junior Cert., eight A's and three B's, he deserved to do well as he'd worked so hard to get these results. Both Maura and Stephen were extremely proud of him, and it looked like his dreams of going to university would become a reality; if he maintained these grades, and there was no reason why he shouldn't. He was considering his options regarding what subjects he should concentrate on, with a view to studying architecture in university; mathematics and technical drawing would be useful and so would physics, all of which he excelled at already. Sarah was making good progress, though maybe not quite as well as her brother, she was however, more artistic than Sean. Of course the fact that Sarah was very young when she started secondary school could have a bearing on her grades, and she was the youngest in her year.

Maura had yet to make arrangements to go out with the girls; she was so tired at the end of each day that she couldn't even consider going out socialising; at least not yet. The thought of a night out was tempting and Maura decided that in another month or two she should be able to take some time out from running the two companies; she was in danger of running herself ragged. She also thought that at the end of next month she would be in a position to offer her designers the chance to buy 'Home Comforts'. It would be hard to turn her back on the company that she'd started from scratch, a company that had exceeded all her hopes, in its growth and financial returns. Maura had more than enough to keep her going work wise, and selling 'Home Comforts' made more sense now then it ever did.

Stephen's blunders, if they had to come, couldn't have come at a better time, if that's what you'd call it.

Maura was getting on very well with Niamh, though she never confided in her, not like she had with Jean, once bitten twice shy. Stephen had received two further phone calls from her, each time she asked him to talk to Maura, to make her understand that she'd meant no harm by keeping quiet over his business. He told her that it wouldn't make any difference, no matter what he'd say to his wife, she never listened to him, and Jean of all people should know that. After the second phone call Stephen told Jean that it would be better if she didn't call him again; he didn't want to keep any more secrets from Maura. He had mentioned Jean's first call, to his wife but she had been so annoyed at the audacity of her that she forbid him to talk to the ex-housekeeper. Stephen knew that if Maura got wind of the second phone call his life wouldn't be worth living, despite the fact that it wasn't his fault. He didn't really know why she would want to keep phoning him any way; she wasn't looking to get her job back, so there was no reason for her to ring again. Life was just settling down at home and the last thing he wanted to do was to upset the apple cart, he wasn't going to get another chance if he blew this one. Maura had tied up nearly all the loose ends regarding the selling of 'Home Comforts', and her solicitor and accountant had gone over all the paperwork, everything was in order.

When Maura called the girls into her office and told them of her plans for the sale of her company, she didn't get the reaction she'd expected. Holly burst out crying, thinking that this meant that their friendship would come to an end, and Ciara was afraid that she'd be out of a job. Sinead was the only one who appeared to give it some serious thought, she realised that there was a possibity that one of them might be in a position to buy the company. Maura could almost see her brain working overtime, Sinead would have been her first choice to take over the company. The girls calmed down when they realised that this wasn't the end of the world, or even the worst thing that could happen to 'Home Comforts'. Maura told them that they were being given first refusal to buy the company, lock stock and barrel, and if any of them were seriously interested she would be in her office all day, they could come and talk to her there. Money of course, wouldn't be discussed unless anyone was really interested, though Maura was willing to consider any reasonable offer. The only one who took Maura up on her offer to discuss the possibility of buying the company was Sinead.

The company was in a very good state, as Sinead already knew from working there, and finance wasn't going to be a problem; like Maura, her parents had left her very well off when they died three years previously. Sinead had agreed with Maura that the company was a good investment; now all she needed to do was to consult with her accountant before agreeing to buy 'Home Comforts'. Maura was glad that Sinead was genuinely interested in purchasing her business, and she thought that she would make a great go of it, if the deal went ahead. Naturally Holly and Ciara knew that was why Sinead was spending so much time in Maura's office, but they hadn't time to wait around to hear what transpired. Both designers were busy working on separate projects, but they agreed to meet up that evening to find out what happened in Sinead's meeting with Maura. The office staff wouldn't have taken any notice of Sinead and Maura being in conference all morning; this was usual when new work came in to the office. By lunchtime the two women had covered just about everything and decided to go to lunch together, again this wasn't unusual and no one would jump to any conclusions. Over lunch they discussed getting back in to the swing of their Friday night escapades, they would still keep in touch no matter who bought the company, and agreed that meeting on Friday nights was the best way to do this. Besides which it would still take some time to finalise any deal, there was always a mountain of paperwork to go through. Sinead was excited at the prospect of owning her own company and she couldn't wait to tell the girls that they might actually be looking at their new boss. Of course she still had to set up a meeting, to arrange financing, with her accountant; but she didn't foresee any problems there. For the rest of the afternoon, she was walking on air, and she didn't get much work done, she was way too excited. Maura had asked Sinead to keep their discussions private until they had something concrete to go on; of course this didn't include Holly and Ciara who were very discrete and completely trustworthy. Maura knew that Sinead would want to tell her best friends what she was hoping to do, and she herself thought that they would be delighted that the company would be in good hands. That night Maura thought about telling Stephen about Sinead's proposal, it had been a while since she'd shared any information with him; but she changed her mind she didn't want to put a jinx on things. Sinead met with her mates that night and both girls said that she'd make a great boss, though Holly was a little envious, and wished it could be her with the money to buy the business. Ciara thankfully was over the moon for her friend, she would have no problem taking orders from Sinead and she said so.

Everything was falling nicely in to place, Sinead was going ahead with buying 'Home Comforts' from Maura, and now that it was going through Holly and Ciara were pleased for Sinead. The three friends and Maura had started going out again on a Friday night, just to a popular watering hole in town, and everyone was happy. Maura felt good going out again, it was nice to have a reason to dress up in her glad rags, and even the children seemed pleased for her; she deserved a night out. They were at an age now when they wondered why their parents slept in separate rooms, and why they never went out anywhere together. They never questioned their father but Maura was constantly being asked all sorts of personal questions, which she managed to evade most of the time. Sarah was the most inquisitive, Sean was too busy studying to ask many questions, and he already knew most of the answers. Sarah, on the other hand behaved more like an eighteen year old than her thirteen years, of late she had become quite rebellious and if the truth was known she was quite obnoxious for one so young. At times Maura despaired of her daughter's behaviour, which had a very disruptive effect on the family, and she could be extremely argumentative and generally badly behaved. Her mother couldn't understand why she always seemed to be spoiling for a row; she missed her good-natured little girl and wondered where she'd gone. Whenever she tried talking to Sarah she got very upset and promised to mend her ways, there would be a lot of tears and things would generally improve for a few days; inevitably the improvement was short lived. Maura blamed her daughter's mood swings on puberty and the raging hormones of adolescence, she was grateful that Sean hadn't been as difficult as his sister. Stephen didn't seem to notice the change in his daughter's behaviour; he was too busy trying to keep on the right side of his wife. All through their married life Stephen had left Maura to deal with their children, secretly he thought that it was the woman's job to bring up the children. Of course he was cute enough not to say anything like this to Maura; she'd eat the head off him if he did. Maura asked her son if he'd noticed a change in his sister but he hadn't; Sean didn't see much of Sarah any more, not even at school, as much of his time was spent in the library. His mother asked him to keep an eye on her at school to see if she was mixing with the wrong crowd, and she told him that she would talk to Sarah's teachers at the next parent/teacher meeting. Sean agreed to look out for his little sister, they'd always been so close in the past; now he couldn't remember when he'd last had a proper conversation with her, he vowed to change that.

Maura was glad that she'd had a good chat with her son; it was a pity that she couldn't have a decent conversation with his father, and it was times like this when she really missed her parents. She'd always been able to talk to them, no matter what the problem might be, she had no one now except her son, who she didn't want to burden with unnecessary worries. Maura needed a man in her life, a proper man; not just one for sex, though come to think of it she wouldn't be averse to that. She thought that there must be a way of meeting a nice, sexy, uncomplicated man, who'd make her feel special for a change. Maura repeated her thoughts to the girls on the Friday night, when they met up in town. Ciara suggested speed dating which was very popular, Holly disagreed, and she said that a personal ad in the Evening Standing might be her best bet. Sinead thought for a while before suggesting that they all join a salsa dancing class, she had always fancied learning a sexy dance like that. There were sure to be plenty of available men there and if there weren't they could still have a good time and get fit at the same time. Maura smiled at Sinead, this idea appealed to her, it did sound like fun; and if there were a few men thrown in then all the better.

The salsa classes were on a Thursday night and the four friends joined up for the beginners course, consisting of eight one-hour lessons, over eight weeks. Sinead had been right; the classes were fun; though there weren't many eligible men there. Maura didn't really mind, and she had no intention of going to a speed dating night, no matter how desperate she became. Her vibrator would need new batteries, as it looked like it would have to come out of retirement. The classes were great craic and they went for a few drinks afterwards, their Friday nights were put on hold for the duration of the dance lessons. Maura benefited most from the dancing, she put her heart and soul into it, and she felt the benefit to her health; she had more energy than before. She had always looked after her figure and now she was even more toned, Stephen had noticed how well she looked. Of course he was convinced that she was having an affair, why else would she be in better form and look much happier lately.

The sale of 'Home Comforts' went through without a hitch, and the new owner, Sinead, organised champagne and nibbles for the office staff, who had been a bit peeved to have been kept in the dark until the last moment. The champagne went a little way to appease their pride, plus the personal apology from both Sinead and Maura seemed to pacify them. Maura took her three designer friends out for a farewell meal on the night that the contracts were signed. There was a great atmosphere in the pub, which had a mixed clientele, varying in age from around twenty to fifty years. Maura was going to miss going to work, she'd miss the camaraderie; she would miss having any one to confide in. They would still continue to meet up once a week, but it wouldn't be the same any more; Maura would be on the outside, no longer privy to the day-to-day goings on. The girls said that they'd always include her, but
· Maura knew that wouldn't be feasible; besides which Maura

didn't intend sitting on her backside at home, for the rest of her life. Maura had plans; plans that were only in her head right now, but they were plans just the same. She remembered that this was the way that 'Home Comforts' had started, it too had started off as a plan in her head. They were all a little tipsy and tearful by the end of the evening, Maura more so than the rest; which was probably down to her age, she couldn't drink as much as she used to.

Stephen had been dreading the day that Maura would sign over her company to its new owner; he knew that this would leave her more time to concentrate on his. He still thought in terms of the painting and decorating company as his, after all he had run it for much longer than his wife had. A woman shouldn't run a painting and decorating business as far as Stephen was concerned that was a job for a man. He had almost forgotten the mess he'd got into while running it himself; Maura hadn't. On a rare occasion Maura considered handing back the reins to Stephen, to give him another chance; then she'd remember that he wasn't cut out to do that kind of job. Stephen was a good manual worker when he wanted to be, but that was his limit, he hadn't the brains to do a managerial job; it was hard to tell him that.

Sarah was still being a pain in the arse, and at times she was impossible to talk to; Sean hadn't been able to suss out what was wrong with her, but he did try being a friend to her again. He was up to his eyes studying for his Leaving cert, which was coming up in less than six months time; he didn't even get to spend much time with his girl friend, Lisa, who was three months younger than him. At seventeen, Lisa was very mature for her age; she too was very studious, this is what had drawn Sean to her in the first place. The romance had been blossoming over the last few months, but Sean had yet to bring her home to introduce her to his family; he was planning on doing that in the next week or two.

Maura had decided to sign up for the intermediate salsa classes, but she couldn't convince the others to do the same; they hadn't really got the hang of it the way Maura had, she was a natural. She felt slightly guilty that she'd now be out two nights a week, however, she reasoned that her children had their own social lives, so why shouldn't she. Sarah was now going to teenage discos, and from what Maura heard through Sean, she was hanging around with a boy three years her senior. Maura had spoken to her daughter about the birds and the bees, but Sarah told her that they were taught sex education in school, and they already knew about contraceptives and safe sex. Sarah had developed physically over the summer holidays, and she had been getting her periods since she was eleven; she thought she knew it all, no one could tell her any thing. Maura wished that her daughter was still her little girl, but knew that she couldn't stop the growing up period, or make it any easier for her; she was coping better than any one else. For once Stephen seemed concerned that Sarah was dating, or hanging around with an older lad; he thought she was too young to be going out at all. When he brought this up to his wife she was livid, why was he suddenly playing the doting, concerned dad, she wanted to know? She accused him of never having been interested in either of their children before now; and she thought it was too late for him to start now.

When Maura and the girls went out for their Friday night do, she asked them for their opinion on her daughter's friendship with an older lad, there were mixed views from Maura's friends. Two felt that the three-year age gap was nothing at this time, but Sinead alone thought that Sarah was rather too young to be going out at all. At the back of Maura's mind, was a niggling thought that she too, thought the same as Sinead, but she felt powerless to control her daughter's behaviour; and a little afraid to try. Sarah was very strong willed just like her mother. They had a very volatile relationship over the last two years, and Maura tried her best to keep the peace as best she could, even if this meant letting Sarah get her own way a lot of the time.

The intermediate dance class had a different crowd of people attending it; and there was only one woman from the beginners group that joined it, along with Maura. This new group were very good and there just happened to be one or two interesting looking men, amongst them. They immediately included Maura and the other woman, June, in to their clique. Everyone in the group encouraged the learners to just relax and enjoy themselves, and Maura felt quite at home with them. One of the men, whose name was Steve, seemed to adopt Maura, he was the oldest of the group; but not the best dancer among them. He reminded Maura of her father, so she was quite content to partner him, and they got on well. Maura still enjoyed the dancing, and she always had some story to tell the girls the next night, about the classes. Ciara had stopped going out with them, she was now dating a nice man and she didn't think it was fair on him if she wasn't available to see him on a Friday night. Poor Ciara felt guilty about letting the girls down and they teased her unmercifully about it; secretly they were all pleased for her. Holly wished that she too would meet a decent fellow; she thought that time was slipping by; she didn't want to be left on the shelf, she wanted a husband and children of her own. Maura said that they'd help her to find her soul mate, she knew one or two eligible bachelors who worked with Stephen; she'd give it some thought, she promised Holly. Sinead didn't want to be left out either, so Maura made her the same promise.

Maura's thoughts of starting a new company, buying and selling antique artefacts, was suddenly pushed aside in favour of a new plan that was taking form in her mind. For the time being she wasn't going to mention it to any one, she needed to give it a lot more thought. Some of Maura's thoughts weren't very practical and she often had to go back to the drawing board several times before coming up with a workable solution; she wasn't easily put off though. At her next dancing class, Maura was more interested in talking to the other single members of the group, than actually doing any dancing; she took note of everything they said, in regards to dating. Maura had come to the conclusion that there weren't many places, outside the pubs, to meet other singles. So the idea of setting up a proper dating agency, which was more concerned with matching up the right people, than with making money, was formulating in her mind. Maura wanted people to have a safe place to meet up with other similar people, people from a similar background and of a similar age group. It would need a great deal more thought put in to it but Maura thought she was on to a winning formula; she would do some more informal research before telling any one of her ideas. She loved it when things came together, she had a great imagination, which helped her to see any drawbacks there might be in her projects. Maura thought about the type of people that she herself would be interested in meeting, and then she thought about where these people would likely be found. She came to the conclusion that in her age group, the majority of them were likely to be married. This led to the question of where would the few unmarried people, in her age group go to meet similar people. Clubs and pubs weren't really the ideal places to meet the person of your dreams, not when you were a person of a certain age group. So Maura thought about the problem for a little longer, and she thought that it would be a good idea if you were introduced to people through other people.

The next problem was where would you go on a 'date' with these other people, and it would have to be somewhere where you would feel the most relaxed; which in Maura's opinion would be at home. Her ideal 'date' therefore would be with a group of like-minded people in someone's home having dinner, what better way to get to know someone then at a dinner party. Maura was very pleased with her deductions, now all she needed to do was sort out the finer details; because of course she wasn't going to have a group of strangers in her own home. There were a lot of possibilities as to where the dinner parties could be held; they could be in a small hall or even in a small private room in a hotel, there were other places to hold parties as well. Maura was anxious to hear what her friends might have to say about her ideas, before she committed herself to this project. Out of curiosity, Maura ran the idea by Stephen; he thought that she was trying to tell him something, and he wasn't at all enthusiastic. To Maura this meant that it could be a very good idea, her husband wouldn't know a good idea if it jumped up and bit him on the bum. If her friends liked the idea, then she knew she was on to a good thing, they would be honest with her; of that she was certain. She was also planning on giving her salsa friends a brief outline of her ideas, in order to gauge their opinions, and as they were a very mixed group she should get mixed reactions.

Maura was beginning to get excited about her possible venture, she was very pragmatic, if this didn't work out then she could always go back to her original idea; buying and selling antiques. Admittedly this wouldn't bring her in to contact with as many people as at a dinner party, though in the long run it could mean meeting some very interesting people, she'd reserve judgement until she had got some other views. Maura wasn't in any hurry.

Chapter 12

This new project was proving to be quite problematic, not least of all because it was difficult to find the right media to advertise in. The girls hadn't exactly given their blessing to the project; they couldn't see how Maura would be able to get the right class of person to attend the dinners. If Maura advertised for professional people to take part in her dinner parties, then she was in danger of getting the wrong type of professional; pro as in prostitute might misconstrue the advert. Maura wasn't having much luck either, in getting together a portfolio of places to hold her parties; so far she only had two venues to choose from, this would need to be expanded in order to make it work. It might be all right to start off with, but it wouldn't look very professional, if it remained at just the two venues. Maura was beginning to lose interest; there seemed no end of obstacles in front of her, and every time she solved one, two more cropped up and she questioned whether it was worth it or not. It wasn't like Maura to fail at the first hurdle, but she just wasn't making any progress; it might be time to call it a day. When she thought about the antiques business, she knew that she didn't have enough experience in that department either, being keen was one thing but with only a limited knowledge, she knew that wasn't going to be the business for her either. Maura became a little downhearted, she wasn't used to things not working out for her, and she needed something to keep her mind sharp. The painting business was now back on course and it didn't take up all of Maura's time. Niamh was working out well; even Stephen grudgingly admitted that she was as good as Jean, if not better. The household didn't need Maura to be there full time, and she couldn't do Sean's studying for him, and she couldn't get through to Sarah to make her see that she should buckle down at school and do some work for a change. Sean's Leaving Cert. exams were looming and he didn't need the added worry over his young sister. Sarah was almost finished her second year but she spent little or no time studying, Maura thought that she shouldn't have let her go to secondary school at such a young age. At the time Sarah was far ahead of the others in her class at national school, and she really wanted to be near Sean, so it seemed like a good idea then. Sarah was mixing with girls and boys at least a year older than herself.

At the parent teacher meeting, it was suggested that Sarah stay back a year, she wasn't ready to sit the Junior Cert. next year; in fact she was very behind in her work. Her teachers hadn't really any good things to say about her, since going in to second year her work had slipped. But worse still was her behaviour, she was insolent and moody and very uncooperative. When she was at home her behaviour remained exactly the same as it was at school, Maura had tried talking to her, but to no avail, Sarah was out of control. If Maura barred her from going out on a school night she just ignored her, in desperation Maura asked Stephen to talk to her. This didn't have the slightest effect on her, Sarah was laughing at him behind his back, and in truth he didn't know how to talk to a teenage girl;

even if she was his daughter. On one of Maura's Friday nights out, with the girls, she confided in them about the trouble she was having with Sarah. The girls all knew Sarah, and they were shocked to hear of her bad behaviour, Sinead was more concerned than Holly. Maura asked them for any advice they could give her, Sinead hated to mention the obvious, but could Sarah be taking drugs? Was it possible that Sarah was on some kind of drugs, ecstasy or something? Maura was quite annoyed at Sinead that she could even think such a thing, but at the same time, a little doubt crept in. No, Maura thought, it wasn't possible, her daughter wasn't even fourteen years old, and she couldn't be on drugs, surely not. Maura thought that if Sarah was experimenting, that she would know about it; and if she didn't then Sean would. The thought that her little girl could be in serious trouble didn't bear thinking about, to Maura it meant that she was a failure, not to mention what it would mean for Sarah. Maura would get to the bottom of it and sooner rather than later, she'd have to be cagey, otherwise Sarah would have her guard up. Maybe Sinead was barking up the wrong tree, maybe there was another reason for Sarah's behaviour; this hope kept Maura from despairing altogether.

When Sean came home from school Maura called him in to the office, she told him that she had suspicions about his sister taking drugs; Sean didn't seemed half as surprised as Maura thought he'd be. When Maura mentioned to him that she'd expected a different reaction from him, he said that he thought Sarah's boyfriend might have introduced her to something. Something? Maura didn't know what 'SOMETHING' meant, she was getting more agitated, drugs had never been a part of her life, and she hoped they weren't about to become a part now. Sean felt sorry for his mother, she had always done what she thought was best for him and his sister, but they could have done with a little more constructive guidance in their lives. Sean wasn't blaming his mother entirely for what might be going on with Sarah; his father had to take some of the responsibility too. As yet they didn't know for certain that Sarah was on any drugs, better they find out before accusing her; without proof they should keep their suspicions to themselves. Maura realised that they were treating this as a forgone conclusion that her daughter was doing drugs, and this wasn't fair to Sarah. Maura did a lot of soul searching and she came to the conclusion that she hadn't been a very good role model for either of her children; she was lucky that Sean had turned out so well. Her next job would be to find out for certain if her daughter was on anything, she phoned her G.P. who was also a family friend, and she confided in him her suspicions. Dr Holmes offered to come round that evening, he said he would be able spot any tell tale signs without having to physically examine Sarah. Maura thought that her daughter was cute enough to see through Dr Holmes's charade, she was smart enough in that department. So Dr Holmes gave Maura a brief description of what to look for, without being obvious. At dinner that night Maura couldn't help staring at her daughter across the table from her, she was as subtle as a steamroller. Sarah became very defensive and clammed up straight away, averting her eyes in the process. Well that was a complete disaster, thought Maura, she should have listened to the experienced Doctor, he would have done a better job than her; she acknowledged that she was out of her depth here. Her daughter had left the dinner table and had barely touched her meal; Stephen didn't ask what was going on, he preferred to bury his head in the sand. Maura knew then that she needed some professional help for Sarah; she was convinced by her reactions that she was experimenting with some kind of drugs. Sean had said nothing during dinner, he thought that it was more than likely that his sister was taking drugs, he felt guilty that he hadn't been a better friend to her. Sean should have kept a closer eye on the ones that she was hanging around with, he knew of the reputation of some of these so-called friends. Regardless of the fact that he was now only two weeks away from the most important exams of his life, Sean felt he'd let his little sis down; and he swore, in his own mind to make it up to her. As soon as his exams were finished, Sean told his mother that he'd take Sarah under his wing; he'd get close to her, like they used to be. Maura was proud of her son, and she knew that if any one could help Sarah then it was Sean; she didn't think that a few weeks would make that much difference one way or another. She encouraged Sean to concentrate on his studies, this was more important than trying to sort out his sister's problems, Maura said that she'd look out for her daughter, it was her responsibility not his. This was a relief to Sean, he wasn't too sure what he could have done any way, his hopes of going to university rested with him getting good grades in his exams. Maura put everything on hold while her son got down to some serious studying, and now she thought that they had been panicking needlessly, that they were blowing things out of proportion. Over the following four weeks, everyone tiptoed around Sarah, no one wanted to cause a scene at this time, and as if in response, Sarah appeared to be back to her old self. She seemed to be making an effort not to upset Sean at this time; she was being considerate; the way she always used to be. Maura noticed this change and prayed that it would last, and who knows maybe they'd been mistaken, she may never have been using drugs at all. Besides the tension in the house over Sean's exams, the other little worry was where Sean might go to study architecture. Maura couldn't bear the thought of him going to one of the universities that he applied to in England; Trinity College, in Dublin was by far her first choice, but she couldn't bring herself to bother him with this right now. Maura was grateful to have the old Sarah back, it made life a lot easier for everyone concerned, and she made a silent prayer in thanksgiving for getting her daughter back.

The Leaving cert over, they could all relax, Maura wanted to plan a return trip to Egypt, for the end of the summer, when the weather would be slightly cooler there. Sarah didn't seem so keen, but she didn't dismiss the idea out of hand, Stephen said that he'd like to go with them, that's if they didn't mind; he remembered how much he'd missed them the last time they'd gone there. Maura didn't care if Stephen came or not, it wouldn't spoil the holiday for her one way or the other, and in fact it might actually be good for Sarah to have all her family around her. Sean liked the idea of getting away after the stress of the exams, but he wanted his girlfriend to come with them; Maura agreed, until Sarah said that she wanted her boyfriend to come along as well. After saying that she'd think about it, Maura said that they were going to keep it strictly family only. Sean knew that it was Sarah's fault that Lisa wouldn't be coming with them, but he didn't kick up a fuss about it; he certainly didn't want Sarah's junkie boyfriend on holiday with them. Maura was pleased that Sean hadn't put up any protest; she didn't want to upset the apple cart, so to speak, with Sarah. It was nice to have the peace restored for however long it would last, there were already signs that Sarah was going back to her moody ways, but Maura tried to ignore these warning signs. As yet she hadn't come up with any more ideas for a new business venture, the past few months had put all thoughts of that out of her head. But if things remained peaceful, Maura would put her thinking cap on again; she was getting restless and needed something to take her mind off some of the more depressing aspects of her life. As usual, Maura's main concerns appeared to be for herself and not for her daughter who was still very young to be going through such an unhappy phase in her life.

Sarah's boyfriend was the only one who understood her; he knew what she was going through with her selfish family. He was always there to help take away the pain, he could always make her feel good about herself, make her forget about her dysfunctional family; he was there for her. He didn't treat her like a child, the way her mother did, and he didn't smother her like Sean did, and he didn't ignore her the way her father did; she trusted him to look after her.

There were great celebrations in the Breslin house, on the day that the Leaving Certificate results were issued. Sean was relieved to find out that he had gained enough points to get in to Trinity College, Dublin, to study architecture. He'd already been offered a place pending the outcome of his Leaving Cert. results. His parents, especially his mother, were extremely proud of his achievements, considering the hassles that had gone on in his home, over the previous year. To get 7 A's and 1 B had required immense dedication on his behalf and he truly deserved to be offered the place of his choice. Maura had booked a course of driving lessons for her son, he already had the basics but an intense course would help him to get a full driver's licence. When this was achieved, Maura intended buying him his first car, she didn't think that he'd have any problems passing his test. On hearing this, Stephen remarked that she was being a bit extravagant, and considering that there would be college fees to pay in a few months, he felt she would be better leaving the car until Sean had finished studying. Maura told her husband, that when he had to start paying for these things, out of his own pocket then he would be entitled to have a say in what was bought for Sean or Sarah. She was fuming, how dare he criticise her for wanting to give the children a good start in life, and it wasn't costing him a cent; she'd spent enough on him in the past. Sean had earned a little treat, he'd never asked for much and he had been a great help in dealing with Sarah, which was more than could be said of her own father; who had been worse than useless.

Maura was fed up listening to Stephen snivelling and whingeing about how no one had ever bought him a car for doing well in exams; Maura pointed out that he hadn't done well at school, so she didn't know what he was going on about. He seemed to be forgetting that anything he did have, he owed to his wife and her parents, if it had been left up to Stephen they'd be bankrupt by now. That put Stephen in his place, he hadn't expected such an outburst from his wife, and he thought that these days she was even harder to talk to; he was sorry he'd said anything. It never occurred to Stephen that his wife might have a point; he was thick skinned over her remarks about it being her money that paid for everything. In Stephen's eyes he was the provider, after all he did go out to work each day, and he did earn money; admittedly he didn't pay for much out of it, Maura didn't expect him to; she had gone ahead and booked their holiday, they were going for the last week in August and the first two in September. After Stephen's gripe about her buying a car for Sean she now regretted the fact that her husband was going with them. She thought that three weeks was too long to spend in his company, it would be bad enough at home; but in Egypt it would be far worse. Their marriage was at its lowest point ever; Maura hadn't felt so miserable in years, not since Larry had finished with her in fact. Maura hadn't thought about Larry in a long time, and she smiled to herself, remembering the good times they'd had. She didn't think it would be a good idea to contact him again, not after what happened the last time with the solicitor's letter; the thought of that made her cringe. After the trip to Egypt, Maura planned to resurrect her social life, she was too young to be celibate, she was a sensuous woman; though not of late. Maura missed the company of men, and she missed being told how beautiful she was; even if she didn't think it was true, it was nice to be told it. Holly and Sinead were both still looking for Mr Right, Ciara was going to get engaged at Christmas; Maura was feeling left out, she was the only one of them without the prospect of love in her life. At her age it wasn't so easy to meet others in her position, considering that she was married and still living with her husband, might put off any offers she could hope to get. The dinner party idea might well have worked if she'd persevered, but she had totally lost interest in that now, and she hadn't the heart to try again. Maura's life needed spicing up, and maybe she'd meet someone on holiday, she supposed it was always possible.

At Dublin Airport, Maura bought two bottles of Hennessy brandy for the holiday; she used Sean's boarding card for one of the bottles; Stephen said that she could have used his, but Maura said he'd expect to share it if she had. This was exactly what would have happened and now Stephen had to buy his own duty-free; Maura had copped on to his miserly ways over the years. Sarah was sulking, she didn't trust leaving her boyfriend for three weeks, he'd probably get bored waiting for her; and he'd find someone else. He had however given her a couple of E's to tide her over. But he told her that she was on her own if she got caught with them on her; she would live to regret it if she told anyone who'd given them to her. Sarah knew that he had a temper, so she had no intention of ever dobbing him in; he wasn't one to be crossed, and she knew it; she thought that they were in love and that it would last forever. At thirteen, she thought she was grown up, she'd lost her virginity and was now using drugs; and she thought that this was living. Her childhood virtually ended the day her grandparents died, at the time she wanted to die as well; she missed them so much. She thought that her brother missed them as much as she did, but he couldn't do; he was getting on with his life, and he was leaving her behind. There had been a time when they were close, now Sean didn't have any time for her; his girlfriend was more important to him, even her mother didn't care about her any more. Now only her boyfriend cared, but if she was gone away too long he'd stop caring too; life wasn't too good for her at the moment, she wished she could talk to her mother, but she couldn't.

The hotel that they were staying at in Cairo, had mixed up the bookings and instead of being given two twin rooms, they ended up with two doubles. Maura refused to share with her husband, so she shared a bed with her daughter and left Sean to share with his father. Stephen said that she was being stupid, it's not as if he intended jumping on her; he had no interest in sex, and hadn't done for years. Sean was easy-going and didn't mind as long as his father didn't snore, and he promised his father that he'd keep to his own side of the bed; he didn't want to end up with his arm around his father.

Maura wasn't happy with the arrangements but felt that complaining wouldn't get them very far as the hotel did seem to be fully booked. The brandy made the holiday more bearable, or rather made her husband's presence more bearable; and she did get a better night's sleep. It also meant that Sarah couldn't get up to any mischief without her knowing about it; at least this is what she thought and hoped. When Maura passed out at night from the generous amount of alcohol she consumed, her daughter took the opportunity to do a tour of the hotel and find a suitable place to enjoy her 'E'. There were limited places for a thirteen-year-old unaccompanied girl to go, there wasn't a disco in the hotel and the bar was for adults only. Still the grounds of the hotel were secluded enough for her not to run in to anyone, she had ventured out one night and walked around the souk but it was too noisy and too crowded; the hotel was safer too. Maura never once woke up, or noticed that her daughter was missing from the bed and from the room. Sean spent a lot of time talking to Lisa on his mobile, it was an expense that he could do without, he didn't want his mother paying for everything for him; even if she could afford to. Stephen was finding the heat difficult to cope with, he found it hard to sleep at night, and not even the brandy could help; he wished he was back in Ireland. He thought he'd never complain about the rain or the lack of sunshine again; he even missed the greenness of Ireland. The holiday had got off to a bad start and apart from Sean no one else seemed that happy to be in such a wondrous country, The trip to see the pyramids at close quarters was the highlight of their stay in Cairo and they did manage to be suitably impressed; with them all agreeing that they were a sight to behold.

The week went by quick enough and their

accommodation at the Red Sea resort was five star rating, with no mix-ups this time. They swam each day and relaxed either by the pool or by the lagoon, and though it was hotter in El Gouna, there was a pleasant breeze to keep Stephen from grumbling constantly. Most nights they ate in the hotel dining room because Stephen found walking, even in the evening, too much; the temperatures were still up on 30 degrees centigrade at 10p.m. For the umpteenth time, Maura asked him why he'd come with them, he'd done nothing but moan from the time they left their house; he was ruining the holiday for them. Sarah wasn't really taking any of it in so his moaning wasn't bothering her; she wished that she was back in Ireland as well. Maura was well oiled most nights; she said it helped her to put up with Stephen, at least that's what she told her son, who was the only one who was enjoying the holiday. He knew that he had a few hard years of studying in front of him, and he wasn't going to be living at home during that time; there was only so much he could take from his family. He and Lisa had already talked about living together, they were both hoping to study at the same college and it followed that living together made sense. Maura was unaware of her son's plans, not that she'd blame him for wanting to live elsewhere, they didn't exactly have a loving home life, enticing him to stay. Sean didn't want to make any firm plans until they'd checked out the accommodation scene. They wouldn't be short of money, due to the generous trust fund his grandparents had set up for him before they died, but Sean was prudent where money was concerned; he'd learnt from his father's mistakes. He wasn't planning on telling his parents while they were on holiday, he didn't want to ruin what they had left of it.

Maura couldn't wait for the holiday to end, it was such a

disappointment after the last one, and that was all down to her husband's presence; and Sarah wasn't exactly a bundle of laughs either. A singles' holiday might be worth considering, thought Maura, who had been looking forward to the break; but now just wanted it to end, along with her marriage. She felt that there was no point continuing this farce of a marriage; they would have been better off splitting up years ago. If they had done so, then they might all be a lot happier now; better late than never, mused Maura. She knew that if she were to divorce Stephen, she'd have to make some sort of settlement with him, maybe even give him a lump sum to get him out of the business and out of her life. Alternatively, she could hand over the business to him and be done with him and the business altogether. That might be a wrench, seeing as her parents had set it up in the first place, but in the long term it might be the wisest solution; if Stephen failed then he'd have no one to blame bar himself. With her mind made up about a few matters, Maura tried to enjoy the last couple of days of their holiday. They all tried to pretend that they were having a good time, they smiled, and laughed at the others' jokes, but when it came time to return to Ireland they each gave a sigh of relief; pleased to be going home.

Chapter 13

The last couple of days in Egypt were stressful for the whole family, with each having their own agenda, and each pretending to have a good time. The holiday had helped Maura to make her mind up about her marriage, it was over; and soon she hoped to make that official. She would make sure to discuss the financial arrangements with her solicitor, before letting Stephen know the position. Maura didn't feel that she owed him anything but she wasn't totally heartless, she'd see that he had enough to manage on for a certain period of time, then it would be up to him; he'd either sink or swim. Sarah was a different matter, Maura was almost certain that her daughter had taken some illegal substance while on holiday, even if she couldn't prove it, she was going to have to seek professional guidance, if she was to be of any help to her. Sean, Maura knew could take care of himself, so she didn't need to worry about him, she could concentrate on sorting Sarah out and getting her the help she needed. Her first phone call on arriving home was to her solicitor, she made an appointment for the following week, there was no need to rush in to his office immediately; she had plenty of time.

Maura was keen to talk to the girls to see what news they had, if any, she managed to get Holly on her mobile and she filled her in on the recent happenings. Ciara had split up with her boyfriend; she was devastated when she caught him cheating on her, with a man. Sinead had met a seemingly nice fellow at a club that herself and Holly had gone to the night that Maura and co had gone on holiday. Holly was still looking for Mr Right, but was beginning to think he didn't exist, and she wondered if Maura would like to think again about the possibility of starting up the dinner party project. Maura wasn't going to revisit that idea, but she did offer to accompany Holly on any social outings that might be better with a friend in tow. They caught up on the entire goings-on at 'Home Comforts', which was still doing very well under Sinead's ownership. Maura still had a little pang of envy that she wasn't still involved in the company, though she sincerely hoped that it would continue to thrive for Sinead. The two women made arrangements to meet up on the Friday night, with Holly promising to get the other women to join them, at least for a drink. This gave Maura something pleasant to look forward to. Sinead rang her to say she'd love to meet for a drink and could she bring her new boyfriend, she wanted to show him off to her best friends. Sinead had only just met him, but she was already head over heels in love with him; he was a few years older than her and was separated from his wife, thankfully they had no children. Sinead hadn't even told him what she did for a living, she was playing it ultra cool, and she was hoping to appear mysterious, her new man seemed happy to play along. Maura admired her tactics, she'd never have thought of doing anything like this herself; she had to admit that it could be fun if you got into the spirit of it. Ciara had also said she'd like to meet up with them, she was still reeling about her ex's bisexuality, her confidence had taken a battering; she'd loved him so much. Stephen was back at work; the lads who worked for him had apparently worked harder while he'd been away. Maura still hadn't told Stephen what she was planning to do with the business, she wasn't sure if giving it to him lock stock and barrel was the right thing to do. Before they'd gone on holiday, Maura had talked to the apprentices who worked with Stephen, and she'd promised them a bonus if they worked like Trojans while they were in Egypt. It looked as if her bribe had paid off, she had asked them not to tell her husband, or the deal was off; the incentive had worked and the backlog of jobs was cleared. She wondered why her husband couldn't achieve the same results, a little incentive would go a long way, and the company would be in a much better shape. Sarah had missed the first two weeks of the new school term, she was staying back to repeat second year, and she was not one bit happy about this. Maura told her that she'd make new friends in that year and maybe if she caught up with the work then she might be allowed to rejoin her old classmates. This wasn't entirely true, but Maura thought it might encourage her daughter to study more, unfortunately it made her more rebellious. Sarah hadn't heard from her boyfriend since going to Egypt, she'd tried phoning everyday, without success, and she was sure that he'd found himself another girlfriend. Of course she blamed her mother for not letting him come on holidays with them, she didn't find out for another week that he'd had to flee the country; he owed some nasty characters a lot of money and they wanted it back. In some ways this appeased Sarah, she knew that he must have had a good reason for not contacting her. One of his cronies had got a message to her, he needed at least five thousand euros and he was banking on her to get the money for him. Sarah wasn't able to touch her trust fund, which had been set up for her by her grandparents and the only other way to get the money was by stealing it. She knew that there was always quite a large sum of money kept in the office, and she knew where the key was kept. If she got caught she'd be in big trouble, but she felt she'd be able to lie her way out of it, she might even be able to put the blame on Niamh, who she'd never really taken to. Sarah had to choose her time carefully, the key belonging to the office was always kept in the drawer of the kitchen dresser, and she'd have to wait for Niamh to go upstairs before she could get her hands on it. Her chance came when Niamh went to change the bath-towels, and she slipped in and took the key from the dresser, she still had to wait for the housekeeper to go home before going to the office. Sarah was quite excited about what she was about to do; it would be the first time in her life that she'd done anything like this. As soon as Niamh had left Sarah went into the office, she managed to open the small safe even though her hands were shaking and her heart was pounding; there wasn't the amount of money there that she needed, and she almost burst in to tears. She thought that if she took some of her mother's jewellery she might be able to make up the balance, she could take it to a pawnbroker, or somewhere else. Sarah didn't have a clear idea what she was going to do, and she decided to put the money back for the time being; if her mother discovered it missing she'd have a harder job getting the rest. She had only just put the key back in its rightful place when her mother returned home from a shopping trip, she had enjoyed the adrenaline rush but she would have to be more careful in future. Maura wondered why Sarah was hanging around the kitchen, her daughter looked a little flushed, and might be coming down with something, she hoped not. Missing school was the last thing that Sarah needed, she would never catch up at this rate, and Maura regretted keeping her off school while they were on holiday, not the most sensible thing to do. It wasn't as if they'd even had a good time, and if she got sick now it would be the last straw. Sarah barely spoke to her mother when she asked her if she was feeling alright, she went upstairs to her bedroom, slamming the door as she went. Maura was coming to the end of her tether with Sarah; she was going to ask Dr Holmes to refer her to a counsellor, who might be able to help her.

When Maura contacted the family doctor, he was surprised to hear of all that was going on in their lives, he was especially saddened to learn about young Sarah's involvement with drugs; she was only a child. He certainly hadn't been expecting to hear that drugs had touched the lives of the Breslin household, but then he shouldn't be surprised at anything these days. He suggested that he talk to Sarah himself, she might tell him what had started her on this road, and there was usually an underlying reason for someone as young as Sarah to get involved with drugs. It wasn't as if she came from a broken home, and she certainly wasn't a deprived child, no, he thought there was some other likely explanation. Maura wanted an expert, someone who knew what they were talking about and she didn't think that Dr Holmes was likely to have had that much experience of drug abuse. However she was willing to let him talk to Sarah if he felt he could do some good, she didn't know how Sarah would take it; she hoped she wouldn't throw a tantrum. The appointment with Dr Holmes was made for the Friday evening; Maura would need an outing if things went badly. Maura decided to leave telling Sarah about seeing the doctor until the actual day, it would give her less of a chance to get out of going, and she wouldn't have time to come up with an excuse not to go. Sean was working with his father until college started in a few weeks time, his mother had thought it was a good idea, it got him out of the house; he was happy to help out and didn't complain. Maura wished that his sister was more like him, he had never caused her a moment's worry and God knows he had the same upbringing as Sarah, but he was a totally different kettle of fish. Why couldn't they be more alike? Sean hadn't tried drugs, at least not to her knowledge and he had brains to burn; Sarah too had plenty of brains if only she'd use them.

Niamh had left a roast chicken in the oven, and it was ready to carve, Maura had cooked the vegetables and was just waiting for Stephen and Sean to arrive home. With the table set and the dinner cooked, Maura poured herself a brandy; it was at this time of the day that she really enjoyed a drink. In ten minutes the peace would be disturbed, and her husband and son would come in from work starving, and Sarah would make an appearance, with a sour look on her face. Maura knew the routine and prayed that for once Sarah would prove her wrong; it would be great to have a meal in a relaxed atmosphere for a change. They never seemed to have a proper chat over dinner, not like they used to, and with Sean being out at work during the day Maura never got a chance to catch up with him. Soon he'd be at college and they'd have even less time to chat, he still hadn't told his family that he was looking for a flat for himself and Lisa, he knew his mother would take it much harder than his father. Maura finished her drink just as the men arrived home; she put her glass in the dishwasher and proceeded to serve up the dinner. Right on cue Sarah appeared at the kitchen door Maura turned and smiled at her, she got a scowl in return, but she didn't let the smile drop from her face; she wasn't going to let Sarah get to her. Maura thought that it was a sad day when she dreaded her daughter's company at the dinner table. She tried hard to stay cheerful, which wasn't easy; she felt such a failure as a mother despite having such a great son. Where had she gone so wrong with her little girl? Maura left the dinner table without eating anything, she poured herself another brandy and took it upstairs to her bedroom; she didn't say a word to anyone, as she choked back the tears.

Sarah's appointment with Dr Holmes went exactly how Maura expected it to go, badly. Her daughter had ranted and raved at her before finally giving in and going, she knew that she didn't have to cooperate with him, and it might get her mother to leave her alone from now on. Dr Holmes got the distinct impression that Sarah's unhappiness at home had been one of the reasons why she'd gone off the rails. She was a very troubled young girl, and it was obvious that she'd need professional help and as soon as possible. He made an appointment for her to see a counsellor on the Monday, following her visit to him, it was lucky that her parents could afford it; it made getting an appointment straight away possible. Money did talk in some cases. Sarah was still trying to get her hands on the money for her boyfriend, it wasn't proving as easy as she had thought it would, she'd tried the safe again but this time there wasn't any money in it at all. It was hard to find out where the money had gone, she couldn't just ask her mother; she'd have to come up with another idea to get the money. Over dinner she heard her mother asking her father for some money for her night out with the girls, she'd taken the money from the office to the bank and she'd forgotten to keep some for her personal needs. Stephen said that he'd been paid in cash for one of the jobs he'd done and that he'd put the money in the safe just before dinner; Maura said she'd take some of it and she'd leave an IOU to remind herself to replace it. She wanted to make sure that the books were kept straight; she didn't want to do a 'Stephen' on them. Maura was really glad to be getting out that night, she needed some adult company for a change, and she was looking forward to catching up with the girls. They were meeting up in The Hagen pub at 8 o'clock and Maura was running late, so she phoned for a taxi; normally she'd catch a bus from the end of the street, it took her right to the door of the pub. Sarah had watched her mother get in the taxi, and then she went into the kitchen to get the office key, which was where it should be. Her father was upstairs taking a shower and Sean had gone out to meet his girlfriend, which left the way clear for her to get the money from the safe. Once again, Sarah's heart was pounding as she let herself into the office and opened the safe; this time there was a lot more money there. Sarah's conscience didn't bother her, as she counted out five thousand euro; she only took the amount that her boyfriend needed to get him out of trouble. She had only closed the office door when her father came in to the kitchen and in her haste she forgot to lock the door, before she replaced the key in its rightful place. Sarah knew that she'd have been able to front it out with her father, but he would have told her mother, who would have known she was up to something; the office was always out of bounds to her and her brother. Stephen didn't notice that his daughter was behaving strangely or that she'd just come out of the office, he was getting a can of Guinness for himself and was looking forward to watching some football on the television. Sarah went back to her bedroom to phone her boyfriend's contact, the sooner she got the money to him the sooner her boyfriend would be back to her. She arranged to meet him later that night. She'd have to sneak out once her father was in bed, she knew her mother wouldn't be home until late; Sean would probably stay at Lisa's, which would make it easy enough to get out. It seemed to take forever for her father to go to bed and she'd almost fallen asleep while waiting, quietly she tiptoed downstairs and went out the front door. She wasn't meeting her contact far from her house, as it was too risky for her to be out late at night carrying so much cash with her. When she paid over the money, she asked when her boyfriend would be able to return to Dublin and was told that he'd be back before the weekend was over. This news put a smile on her face and she was told that he'd be in touch the next morning. Sarah raced back to her house and sneaked back in, getting in just before her brother Sean; Sarah hadn't expected him to come home that night but luckily she got in before he did. Sean wouldn't have gone home if he hadn't fallen out with Lisa; she was pushing him to get an apartment for them in an expensive area of Dublin, which was too far from college. Sean didn't mind the cost, but he didn't want to spend a couple of hours travelling to and from college every day, it wouldn't leave him enough time for studying. Lisa should understand, after all she was going to have to make the same journey with him; he couldn't understand what was wrong with a flat near the campus. That would make it a lot easier for them both, but Lisa was digging her heels in over the area in which they should look to live in; she could be so stubborn when she didn't get her own way. Sean saw that there was a light on in Sarah's room so he went in to have a quick chat with her, she was still dressed, she said that she'd been doing her homework and had only just finished. Somehow Sean didn't think she was telling the truth, there wasn't a book in sight and her computer wasn't switched on, but Sean didn't want another argument that night.

While they were talking they heard their mother come in, she too was home early and Sarah knew she'd been lucky not to get caught. Once the money was discovered missing, Sarah was likely to be the prime suspect and she knew that. Maura wasn't in a good mood after her night out, and she hadn't expected to see her daughter's light still on or Sean there; she would have preferred not to have to talk to anyone that night. She checked on Sarah to see what was keeping her awake, but she was told, sarcastically, that she was just doing what she'd been told to do; studying. Sean gave his sister a prod in the ribs, he hated the way she treated their mother, they used to be so close; he wondered why things had changed. Sean said goodnight to his sister, and he and his mother walked to his room. Sean told his mother the full story about why he and Lisa had fallen out, she was surprised that he'd been thinking of moving in with his girlfriend; she didn't know why she hadn't thought that this might happen. Sean was nineteen now, and not many lads his age still lived at home, but now it looked like Maura might have him for another while, if she was lucky. She didn't tell her son why she was home early; she was still shocked at meeting Larry again after all this time.

Sinead had been waiting in The Hagen for her, and her new boyfriend had just gone to the toilet; Maura thought that Sinead looked radiant; this new boyfriend of hers must be the reason. Sinead went up to the bar to get Maura a drink and while she was away her boyfriend came back from the toilet,

Maura was shocked when she realised that Sinead's new boyfriend was 'her' Larry. Maura was sure that Sinead must have met Larry before, when she'd been going out with him, but it turned out that she'd only ever seen him that first night he'd met Maura in the nightclub. Sinead and Holly hadn't been very close to him and didn't get a good look at him; Sinead had no idea that he was 'the' Larry, Maura's Larry. When Larry realised that Maura was one of the friends that Sinead wanted him to meet, he was embarrassed, the last time he'd spoken to Maura was after her parents had died. Sinead came back with the drinks to find her boyfriend and Maura chatting away as if they were old friends, which they had to tell her, they were; there was a moment of embarrassment but it passed quickly. Sinead couldn't believe that Larry and Maura had once been a couple, but she cast her mind back to the time when Maura was going through a hellish phase, this must have been because of Larry. Maura now seemed well and truly over Larry, which was good because Sinead and Larry were besotted with each other. Larry told Maura about his ex-wife, Julie's, miscarriage and how she couldn't deal with it; she'd left him, saying that it was his unhealthy sperm that had kept causing her to lose her babies. Poor Julie, she wouldn't accept that the problem wasn't anybody's fault; it was just an unfortunate quirk of nature. Larry had tried to get her to talk to someone, but Julie went home to live in her mother's old house and since then Larry had been served with divorce papers. Their divorce would become legal in the coming months; this was all news to Sinead who hadn't asked Larry any personal details; besides which they'd only just got together. Maura felt sorry for Larry and Julie, not having children must have really put their marriage under a lot of strain; she hoped that she hadn't added to the strain when she started phoning Larry. He had the decency not to mention that period in their lives, and Maura was grateful for that, she didn't want Sinead to know any of the details. By the time that Holly arrived, she was late as usual, Maura and Sinead had heard Larry's tale of woe. Holly was impressed with Sinead's boyfriend, she wasn't told the full story of his previous association with Maura, and they merely told her that they were old acquaintances. After all Maura had redesigned his house for him, Holly didn't need to know that they'd been lovers as well. Maura wondered if he still lived in the same house, and if Sinead would change it, and maybe revamp it to her taste, Maura had to stop this line of thought; Sinead had only just started to see him. With a migraine threatening, Maura made her exit before closing time, she needed to get some fresh air; meeting up with Larry had upset her. She thought back to the phone call he'd made to her after her parents had died; she wondered if his marriage had broken down then. Maybe he had been trying to get back with her, or maybe not, she told herself that he was with Sinead now and she should put him out of her mind; he was off-limits. Maura walked as far as the next bus stop and caught the bus home, she had hoped that her daughter would be asleep, she hadn't expected to find her son there talking to her. The migraine was an excuse to leave the pub early, Maura very seldom suffered from headaches, though she felt that there was one coming on now.

Maura spent a few minutes talking to her children, Sarah was as sarcastic as ever, and Sean had told her of his plans to move out of home; these plans had now been shelved since his row with Lisa. All Maura wanted to do was crawl into her bed and have a good cry, tonight had been a right kick in the teeth, and she was even lonelier than before. Maura knew she'd have to get over Larry, she wasn't going to try to come between him and Sinead, but she wasn't going to keep joining them on nights out; she wouldn't be able for that. It took her a long time to fall asleep that night, she relived those times when she was seeing Larry; she also recalled the solicitor's letter she'd received. Maura didn't think that he would ever tell Sinead about that, at least she hoped he wouldn't, she was embarrassed enough about that. She supposed that she could always blame it on the grief of losing her parents, when she'd gone a little off her trolley; she didn't want to think about that. With it being the weekend, Maura didn't think she'd have to talk to Sinead before Monday, and Monday was the day that Sarah was to see the counsellor; that was going to be another heart-rending experience, thought Maura.

Chapter 14

Maura hadn't expected Stephen to take Monday off to go with her and Sarah to the psychologist, but secretly she was pleased; she didn't fancy the idea of her being on her own if it turned out that Sarah had serious psychological problems. Not that she'd expect Stephen to be any good in dealing with any sort of problem, but he would be some company for her, and any company was better than no company. Sarah said nothing for the whole trip, she had a way of making her parents feel as if everything was their fault, and they were well used to the silent treatment from her. The appointment was for 10a.m. and Sarah was seen on time. Maura and Stephen accompanied their daughter for the initial introductions and were then asked to wait outside in the waiting room, while Dr Anne Connor talked to Sarah on her own. Maura wasn't too happy about this but she could hardly kick up a fuss without giving her daughter more ammunition with which to attack her with. Dr Connor ordered various tests for her new patient, before settling down to talk to Sarah, or rather to let Sarah talk to her. From her body language alone it was clear that she wasn't happy to be there, but this was usual for new patients to feel defensive and sometimes victimized. It could take some time to get a patient to trust her but she had always managed it in the end.

Sarah decided to try to end the meeting or interview as quickly as possible, by telling the doctor what she thought she wanted to hear, namely about her home life. Sarah rushed through a hackneyed version of her life to date, touching briefly on a few important incidents, which she dismissed as trivial events. Dr Connor had been a consultant psychologist for numerous years and could pinpoint the event that had had a devastating effect on Sarah almost immediately. The tragic death of her grandparents and the subsequent aloofness of her mother had left Sarah feeling partly responsible for their deaths; though totally innocent she had developed an irrational guilt complex. Sarah was unaware of these feelings which culminated in her belligerent behaviour and which her family had blamed on those around her at school. The drug taking wasn't even touched upon during this first appointment, a need to assure Sarah of the confidential nature of these meetings was of paramount importance; the rest would follow as a consequence. Dr Connor was extremely pleased with this initial meeting and she was sure that the prognosis for Sarah was a very good one. A further meeting was scheduled for the following week, but at a later time so as not to disrupt her schooling, and so ensuring that her counselling remained a private matter for Sarah and her family alone. Sarah refused to tell her parents anything that had been said between her and her counsellor, she was quite pleased that they had been excluded from the session. She didn't think that she'd actually said anything of importance during the session but she did feel a little less tense as a result of it, and she made up her mind that she'd go again the following week. Sarah hadn't heard from her boyfriend since giving his mate the 5,000 euros, but she trusted him to get in touch as soon as he could.

Maura and Stephen had sat in silence in the waiting room while their daughter, they assumed, poured her heart out to a complete stranger. Neither of Sarah's parents had any idea what took part in these sessions, but they both agreed that as long as they 'worked' they didn't mind how long it took or how much it cost. They didn't expect to see any change in Sarah's attitude straight away so they weren't disappointed, and they weren't expecting miracles, but they were happy to have passed the problem on to someone else to deal with. They couldn't help having this attitude; they just hadn't known how to cope with their young daughter, and her unreasonable behaviour. Stephen went back to work after he dropped his wife and daughter at home. He had a lot of work to get through, and he was hoping for some good weather so that he could get started on a new job; that of painting the old barracks, on the southside.

Maura let Sarah have the rest of the day off school; she needed to do some paperwork that afternoon and she told her daughter that she'd be in the office for the next few hours. Sarah realised that she was going to be found out if her mother had to open the safe; she'd know that a sizeable amount of money was missing. Maura wouldn't have to be Sherlock Holmes to work out who'd taken the money; Sarah didn't think that she'd be able to convince her mother that Niamh, their housekeeper, was responsible. Sarah decided that she'd be better off going back to school and keeping out of her mother's way, so she got changed into her school uniform and shouted to her mother that she was going back to school. Of course Maura mistook her enthusiasm as having something to do with the session with the psychologist; she was delighted that Sarah was showing some interest in going to school. It was a minor miracle and one that Maura wasn't going to complain about. She got stuck into the paperwork and put the accounts in order; Maura wanted to do something nice for her daughter and thought that a shopping trip at the weekend would be a good idea.

In the evening, Sinead rang Maura for a chat, she wanted to make sure that Maura wasn't still keen on Larry because she didn't want to hurt her, and she was really taken with Larry. Maura and Sinead talked for almost an hour, during which time Maura realised that she was fully over Larry; she wished her friend well in her new relationship. Sinead wanted to meet up again on the Friday night but Maura was able to put her off with some excuse about spending quality time with her children. This gave Maura another idea about going away for the weekend, maybe to the West of Ireland; she didn't think that Waterford would be a good choice. As it was only Monday, Maura decided not to mention the weekend to her family; she'd book somewhere first before telling them. Stephen was talking about some homeless man he'd met, who used to own his own business but had lost everything over not having insurance, Maura just said that he couldn't have been much good then. Stephen had felt sorry for him, but he didn't say any more to his wife, she wasn't interested in anything he had to say. Every evening for the next few days Stephen mentioned his homeless friend when he came home from work. Maura only half listened to him, she had booked herself and her two children into a guesthouse in Westport in County Mayo, for the coming weekend. Sean was happy enough as he would be starting in college in a couple of weeks' time and he wouldn't get much time off once that started. However, Sarah threw a tantrum, she still hadn't heard from her boyfriend and she was afraid that she'd miss him if she was away for the weekend. Maura wasn't going to be dictated to by her teenage daughter and she told her so.

The weekend away wasn't exactly a success story. Lisa had been texting Sean; she was missing him and agreed to look for a flat nearer to the college; and Sarah had received a call on her mobile from her boyfriend. Maura cursed the mobile phone culture, every person she met seemed to be attached to one, and it was hard to have a normal conversation any more. Sarah's boyfriend wanted to know where she was, he'd been calling her at home but got no answer and her mobile number was engaged each time he called; he was not a happy bunny. Maura had been hoping that her daughter would never hear from him again, she blamed him for a lot of Sarah's problems, and it was definitely him who got her started on the drugs. It was impossible to ban her daughter from seeing him; that would only cause her to do it behind her back, Maura felt that she was caught between a rock and a hard place. She too wasn't sad when the weekend was over, what with Sean being lovesick and Sarah being...... she wasn't sure what Sarah was, apart from not being happy. The drive back to Dublin was a quiet affair, no one was interested in making conversation including Maura, she was thinking about Sarah's next session with Dr Connor, the following evening. She did wonder if Stephen would bring her by himself, but she knew she couldn't expect him to take on the sole responsibility. Maura wished that life wasn't so unfair; she'd always thought that she was a reasonably good mother, that is, until Sarah got mixed up with drugs. She was living through every mother's nightmare and her husband didn't seem to think that it was a serious problem, he said that their daughter was too smart to get hooked on drugs.

They were lucky with the traffic that evening and they reached home in time for tea; Stephen had prepared a sort of salad for them, though he was having a fry-up for himself. When they had all sat down to eat, he asked Maura if she'd taken the money, which he'd left in the safe the previous week, as he had promised to pay one of the lads in cash, and it wasn't there. Sarah's face reddened and she felt sick with apprehension, it could only be a matter of minutes before her parents would know what she'd done. Maura told her husband that she had taken the money to the bank on the Friday morning and she'd forgotten to mention it to him. Sarah couldn't believe her luck, her mother mustn't have known how much money should have been there, and she breathed a sigh of relief; she'd had a close shave and didn't want to ever repeat that again. The adrenalin surge wasn't as good as previous times, and when Sarah looked across at her mother she found that she was staring right back at her; Sarah averted her eyes, she couldn't hold her gaze.

Maura wasn't ready for the confrontation that had to take place with her daughter, at least not that night, it would have to keep. Of course if her daughter came clean about taking the 5,000 euros it would go some small way to making it alright. Maura and Stephen always made a note in the ledger of any amount of cash that they put in the safe; otherwise it wouldn't be easy to keep the record straight. So on Friday morning as soon as Maura had checked the safe and the book, she knew of the deficit; there was only one person who would have taken the money, and that was Sarah. There wasn't a shadow of doubt in her mind that her daughter had stolen the money, and Maura had even searched her room while she was at school. Maura had hoped that during the weekend away her daughter might just confess to what she had done, but hoping didn't get her very far. She would wait until after Sarah's visit to the psychologist before tackling her over the stolen money, she might even confide in Dr Connor about what she suspected; or rather what she knew. Sarah went up to her room knowing that her mother knew she had taken the money; she didn't know why she hadn't accused her there and then. Sarah knew that something was brewing, and she didn't think she'd like it when the storm finally erupted. In truth, Maura wasn't really sure how to handle this or what to do or even what to say, she felt so let down by her daughter, it was a physical pain. A pain, that wouldn't go away easily and one that tablets couldn't take away; or even ease. Maura got drunk that night in the hope of getting a night's sleep, which she hadn't had in a long time now, not since her parents had died.

A hung-over Maura couldn't face breakfast; instead she soaked herself in the bath for the best part of an hour until she felt almost human. Stephen saw Sarah off to school so as to give his wife a break, he'd heard her getting up during the night and he even thought he'd heard her getting sick. He'd noticed that she was drinking a fair amount of brandy the previous evening, which wasn't unusual, but the speed at which she drank it was. Stephen guessed that she had something on her mind but not what it was; he didn't really want to know in case it was to do with him. He called up to Maura to let her know that he was going to work; he said he'd be home at the usual time that night. Maura phoned Niamh and said that she wouldn't need her until the Wednesday, but of course she would still pay her for the day. She wanted some time on her own, and although Niamh never pried in to their private lives, she was bound to know that something was amiss. Maura never confided in Niamh, she'd learnt her lesson from the time when Jean had betrayed her, she'd vowed then not to make the same mistake again, and she hadn't.

When the phone rang, Maura let the answering machine pick it up but there was only silence, whoever was ringing didn't leave any message, which always infuriated her; why bother to ring if you weren't going to leave a message? Ten minutes later the phone rang again, this time Maura answered it in case it was important, she was shocked to hear the familiar voice of Larry on the other end. Larry had tried ringing her over the weekend but when Stephen answered, he'd hung up without saying anything. Maura asked him if it had been him ringing a short while ago but he said that it hadn't been him; Maura doubted him, it would be a coincidence if it weren't him. However Maura wasn't going to argue with him, she asked him why he was calling her, and she wasn't too amused when he said that he hadn't been able to stop thinking about her since meeting her the week before.

'Does Sinead know that you're ringing me?' asked Maura, sarcastically.

'What do you think?' he answered petulantly, 'I've really missed you,' he continued.

Maura stopped him from saying any more, she reminded him of the solicitor's letter he'd had sent to her, she wasn't going to do the dirty on her friend Sinead, no matter how much it hurt her to reject him. Larry seemed surprised that she wasn't willing to meet up with him some night; he still had some feelings for her even if he had thought that she'd been stalking him a few years ago.

Secretly, Maura was pleased that he still found her attractive, but she had her principles and besides which, she liked Sinead; this would be another secret that she hoped Larry would keep to himself. It was almost time for Maura to get started on cooking the dinner, so she put Larry and his phone call out of her head. The spaghetti Bolognese was cooking nicely when Sean came home from visiting Lisa, he had something to tell his mother about moving into a flat with her, but he didn't want to upset her. His mother helped him to spit it out, she'd known that this was on the books after Lisa had contacted him at the weekend; it was time for him to make the move, and she approved of her. Sean was grateful that his mother was so understanding and she'd even offered to help out with the rent. It was as if she already knew that they had found a flat, even though Sean hadn't mentioned this fact; his mother had a way of knowing these things. When Sarah came home from school, the atmosphere in the house changed, there was a lot of tension; Sean couldn't fail to notice it, this was worse than usual. He decided that he'd have a good chat with his mother, later that night; he wasn't meeting Lisa until tomorrow.

Maura said very little to her daughter, she was finding it very hard not to lose her temper with her, so she avoided eye contact, in the hope of keeping her cool. On the dot of 6p.m., Stephen arrived home for dinner, he didn't notice the strained atmosphere, but then he never noticed a lot of things, when it suited him. As soon as they'd sat down to eat their dinner, he started on again about the homeless fellow he'd taken a shine to; Maura couldn't care less who he'd met, she didn't want to listen to him blathering on, not tonight. Putting her knife and fork down, very carefully, she stood up from the table and without saying a word she went upstairs to get ready to take Sarah to her appointment. Stephen appeared to be the only one who didn't notice Maura's hasty exit from the kitchen, plus the fact that she hadn't eaten her dinner. He had noticed, but he knew better than to make a fuss about it, when Maura went silent that was a sign to him to leave her alone. Stephen hoped to be able to talk to his wife later, he had promised his homeless friend, 'Tommy boy'; that was what he called him; that he'd think about giving him a job, he had to get his wife's approval first though. It galled him that she wouldn't let him make these decisions on his own, that he always had to consult her first. Stephen put Maura's moodiness down to the problems they were having with Sarah, and the session she was taking her to that evening, with the psychologist; things would be better when they'd get home later.

Maura drove in silence; she couldn't trust herself not to say exactly what was on her mind, Sarah prayed that her mother would remain that way. This session with Dr Connor was even better than the first one; Sarah was in such turmoil that she blurted out about taking the money from the safe. The psychologist was pleasantly surprised with Sarah's admission, and she felt her patient would benefit from confessing the same to her mother. It was obvious that Sarah was genuinely sorry for what she had done and confession would clear the way for her to move on. Dr Connor knew that it had taken great courage for her patient to have opened up to her so early on in her counselling, but she knew from experience that this could be a transient phase in her rehabilitation. Dr Connor explained to Sarah why she needed to tell her mother about her reasons for taking the 5,000 euros from the safe; she was pretty sure that the girl's mother already knew who had taken the money. Sarah half-heartedly believed that if her mother knew that she'd taken it; she'd have confronted her before now. Dr Connor was the expert in such matters and she was almost 100% sure that Sarah's mother knew who the thief was. This problem could only be resolved when daughter and mother could face each other with their problems and talk to each other. Dr Connor hoped that by the following session, Sarah would have come clean to her mother; she was a nice girl and she'd be alright, with more counselling sessions.

The drive home was as quiet as the outgoing trip, once or twice Maura thought that Sarah was going to say something, but she fell silent each time. When they got home Sarah went straight to her room, while Maura headed to the sitting room. Stephen was there waiting to hear how they got on. Maura told him that she hadn't been privy to the session and her daughter didn't tell her anything about it. Again Stephen tried to talk to his wife about taking on another worker, Maura wasn't really listening to him, but she told him she'd think about it and let him known the next day. She needed a drink to block out the unhappiness that she was feeling; but tonight she promised herself that she wouldn't get drunk. Stephen fetched a drink for them both, he was sure that his wife would let him give Tom a job, if she didn't he'd have to think up an excuse to tell him in the morning. While they drank their brandies they heard the front door opening and closing; they both assumed that Sean had gone out without saying anything, this wasn't like him. Maura was fuming, when five minutes later Sean walked in to where they were, she knew immediately that it had been Sarah that they'd heard going out and that she must be meeting her no good boyfriend. Sean said he'd heard her mobile ring, and that she sounded angry at whoever was ringing her. Sighing, Maura contemplated following her daughter, but Sean advised against it, instead he said he'd go;

he'd heard where they were meeting, and it might be better if he could talk to her. Reluctantly, she agreed. Stephen went to the kitchen and poured them another brandy, and Maura drank it without saying a word to her husband. After one more drink, Stephen went upstairs to get ready for bed, he seemed to have forgotten that his daughter was AWOL; Maura didn't try to get him to stay up. As usual she was left to deal with their wayward child, and she was sick and tired of having no one to lean on; she was tempted to ring Larry, but she resisted the urge.

It was over two hours later when Sean arrived home with his younger sister in tow; they both looked dreadful, and Maura knew that something awful must have happened. Sean's hand was cut and he had a graze over his right eye, it was obvious that he'd been in a fight; Sarah's face was streaked with tears and she was shaking all over. Maura was suddenly terrified of what might have happened and she screamed at Sean to tell her what he'd done, he was as white as a sheet. Before he could say a word, he threw up all over the sitting room carpet. Maura screamed for her husband to come down straight away, she knew that something serious had taken place and she needed someone to be there with her, even if it was just him. Sean had finished retching by the time that his father appeared beside him and told him to pull himself together, while he fetched a bucket and carpet cleaner. This was the first time Maura had seen her husband clean up after one of his children; he was doing a good job of it. When the vomit had been cleaned up, they all sat down as ordered to by Stephen; for once he was taking charge of the situation. Sean told his parents' that he caught up with his sister in St Stephen's Green, she was arguing with her boyfriend; he appeared to be trying to force her to take something against her will. Sean said that he lost his temper with Sarah's boyfriend, who had been trying to get her to take a couple of E's. Sarah just sat there in between her parents, without interrupting her brother; she had at last stopped shaking. Maura listened as her son continued to tell them the rest of the story. He'd told Sarah's junkie friend to leave her alone, but he just laughed at him, and that's when Sean flew at him and a fight ensued. Sean had eventually got the better of him and knocked him to the ground, where he remained; moaning and clutching his head, and that's where they left him. Sarah spoke for the first time since they'd got home, she said that she never wanted to see him again; she didn't want to take drugs any more, her boyfriend wouldn't take no for an answer. Sarah was crying now, she said that if Sean hadn't come along when he did, her boyfriend would have forced her to swallow the tablets. Stephen and Maura were so relieved that their children had got home safe and sound, albeit a little the worse for the encounter. Sarah had turned a corner, and Maura knew that things were going to get better from now on for her family. She got an ice pack from the freezer to put on Sean's swollen hand, she was proud of him for saving Sarah, she dreaded to think what would have happened if he hadn't gone after his sister. Maura was quite proud of Stephen too, he'd been quite a tower of strength tonight; it's a pity he couldn't be like that more often. It was another hour before they had all had enough, and decided it was time to try to get some sleep, if they could.

Chapter 15

Stephen was the only member of the Breslin household who got any sleep that night; the other family members were too wound up by the events of that evening. He was also the first up the next morning, and for once he was looking forward to going to work. He called his wife with a cup of coffee, she said that she wasn't sure if she should send Sarah to school or not; she'd heard her sobbing during the night but she didn't go in to comfort or console her.

Sean had promised to meet Lisa later that day, they were going shopping for bedding and a few other things for their new flat; but he wasn't in the humour for it now. Maura understood how he felt and she was happy to have his company, it gave her the opportunity to tell him about the missing money; Sean was shocked that his sister could have stolen from her own parents. Now they were both hoping that they could all get back to some sort of normality. When Sarah came downstairs she wasn't dressed in her school uniform, she looked awful, from lack of sleep and her eyes were all puffy from having cried so much. Maura felt pity for her daughter, because she was still just a child in her eyes. Sarah started to explain to her mother why she had taken the money from the safe, she told her the full story of her drug taking and even why she had started in the first place. Once she started talking she couldn't stop. The death of her grandparents and the subsequent aloofness of her mother towards her all played a significant part in her change of behaviour. Both Maura and Sean listened to Sarah's heart-rending account of her loneliness and sense of isolation, and both felt guilt that they hadn't realised how bad she'd felt. Their actions or rather inactions weren't the sole reasons for Sarah's problems; she would have to take some of the responsibility herself.

After Sarah finished admitting her mistakes she begged her mother not to give up on her, and she promised to do whatever her mother told her to in future, even if it meant going to Dr Connor for the next year, she would willingly go for as long as was necessary. Sean left his mother and sister to have a heart-to-heart talk on their own, he was sorry he hadn't been there for his sister, they used to be so close; he'd been too busy getting on with his own life to notice what was going on in hers. Sean walked the short distance to the local newsagent's, he needed to buy some bits and pieces for college, but the headlines in one of the papers caught his eye, and he forgot what he'd gone in for originally. The headlines said that the Gardai were appealing for witnesses to a murder which took place in St Stephen's Green, the previous evening. A drug pusher, who was well known to the gardai, was dead after being beaten about the head. Sean paid for the paper and left the shop. His legs felt heavy and he walked home as if he was in a dream, he didn't remember the walk home.

Sean didn't say a word to his mother when he got home; instead he placed the newspaper on the table in front of her. Maura's face paled as the impact of what she was reading filtered through to her brain. Her first thought was to ring her husband and get him to come home, but she decided to stay calm and not rush into anything. When Maura thought about it for a few minutes, she didn't think that bringing Stephen home from work would help the situation. Part of her brain screamed out to her to ring the Gardai and explain how her son had ended up killing a man. Sean's voice broke into her thoughts when he said that he should go to the Garda Station and tell them what had occurred the night before. Sean wasn't thinking in terms of murder or manslaughter it was just a fight, pure and simple, he didn't realise the gravity of the situation. When Sarah came into the kitchen and saw the headlines in the paper she started crying and saying that this was all down to her, she was the only one to blame.

Maura took control because she knew that Niamh was due there any minute, she didn't want anyone outside of the immediate family to know what had happened. Sarah was despatched to her bedroom, with the pretext that she hadn't been feeling well, and had been kept off school. Sean was told to hide the paper in his mother's dressing table drawer; Niamh wouldn't have any reason to go into her bedroom that day. Maura was unsure what to do next, she considered phoning the family solicitor, but she was worried that he'd feel it was his duty to advise them to contact the Gardai. Before Maura could come to a decision on what to do, her husband rang her, he'd seen the newspaper article in a paper that one of the lads had brought in, and he'd made the connection to his son immediately. Stephen told Maura to do and say nothing; from what he'd read in the paper he didn't think that there was any evidence to link the incident to his son. He didn't think that any of the pusher's associates were likely to cooperate with the authorities; the man hadn't been a popular person in the first place. Stephen wasn't going to come home early, he didn't think that it was necessary, and he wanted to get things finished at work. He'd seen Tommy that morning and he'd given him the good news about him working for him on a trial basis; he hoped that Maura wouldn't change her mind. At work, Stephen gave the impression that he ran the business, it made him feel important and it wouldn't really affect Maura; that's if she didn't know about it. Tommy said that he was really grateful to him for giving him a chance to get his life back together, but he would appreciate it if Stephen would stop calling him 'Tommy' or 'Tommy boy'. Stephen thought this was a bit cheeky of him, considering that he was doing the man a favour; however, he agreed to use the shorter version of his name, 'Tom'.

At home Maura tried to carry on as normal, she made small talk with Niamh, and she kept an eye on her son and daughter. She thought that Sean should keep his arrangement to meet Lisa, it would take his mind off things, but he said he couldn't face it; which was understandable. By the time that Stephen arrived home from work his wife had already decided that the best thing to do for Sean was to take him to the local Garda station and clear up the matter. She thought that the longer they delayed going to the Gardai the guiltier Sean would look, her husband strongly disagreed with her. Stephen was of the opinion that it was best to let sleeping dogs lie; therefore keeping quiet unless forced to do otherwise. When they couldn't come to any satisfactory agreement, they decided to ask Sean and Sarah for their views on what should be done. Sarah was still numb about what had happened and she didn't want her brother to be in trouble for trying to protect her. Sean knew that the right thing to do would be to go to the authorities, but he was afraid that they wouldn't believe that he hadn't hit the pusher very hard; it had to have been the fall that had killed him. So finally they agreed to do nothing for the time being, they'd take each day as it came; they'd play it by ear.

After dinner, Stephen told his wife about taking on the extra man as she'd agreed previously; Maura couldn't remember having agreed to any such thing, but she wasn't in the mood to argue about it. For the following few weeks they read all the newspapers looking for any mention of the 'murder in the park'. After the first two days there was no more mention of it and the Breslin family started to relax, thinking that the murder investigation must have wound down. Each evening Stephen kept Maura up to date on how the new fellow was working out. Stephen was pleased that Tom was a good worker and so far he hadn't let him down; so at least he didn't have to give Maura any more bad news. For once things started to go right for Stephen and he was glad that he'd persuaded his family to sit tight about Sean's fight; he was beginning to feel a bit like a hero. The murder investigation was ongoing and sooner or later a witness was sure to come forward, it was only a matter of time.

As Stephen's confidence at work grew, his son became more introverted; he became shy and preferred to stay at home, rather than go out socially. He saw less and less of Lisa and their plans to share a flat together had been put on hold, due to Sean's lack of interest. Sean had started college, but even that didn't have any effect on his frame of mind, and Lisa knew that their relationship was coming to an end, though she didn't know why. Over the next few months she tried to find out what was bothering Sean, she knew that it must be something serious for it to have changed him completely. Sean wouldn't or couldn't tell her, so she even approached Maura, hoping that she could shed some light on what was wrong with her son and the reason for his total change of character. Maura was quite annoyed at Lisa for her continual questioning of Sean's behaviour, and in the heat of the moment she told Lisa that she was probably too clingy and too needy for Sean's liking. Lisa was gutted. She'd always got on so well with Maura, and now this was like a kick in the stomach, and she knew she didn't deserve it. Sean looked physically ill, he'd lost weight and he had dark circles under his eyes, which obviously meant that he wasn't sleeping well. Eventually in March, Sean and Lisa officially split up, and in a way they were both quite relieved that they had. Lisa wasn't going to forget Sean, and she had made up her mind to find out the real reason for their break-up. There were questions that needed to be answered.

Stephen had been making more and more decisions at work, and Maura seemed happy enough to let him. He hadn't noticed how ill his son was looking or how he never went out any more; he didn't even notice that Sean very seldom spoke. Maura had noticed, but she felt that he would eventually get over the fact that he'd caused the death of a drug pusher. Sarah had applied herself to her schoolwork and was doing very well, she seldom went out socially and Maura was just as pleased that she didn't; she could keep a close eye on her.

Most of the time the Breslin family were tiptoeing around each other and Maura in particular found it very draining. Niamh couldn't help but notice the strained atmosphere in the house and she too felt very uncomfortable, she no longer enjoyed working for the family. After one particular fraught afternoon she gave in her notice. Maura didn't even try to get her to change her mind, and she said that Niamh didn't have to work out her notice, she would pay her up until the end of the month and she'd include her holiday money. Niamh had half hoped that her boss would try to persuade her to stay, and when that didn't happen she was glad to be leaving. When Stephen returned home from work, he said that he wasn't surprised that Niamh was leaving; he said that the whole family needed to pull themselves together. Maura couldn't believe that her husband could be so intuitive, sometimes he amazed her; and she agreed with him, it was time they got their lives back to normal. Sean had to get on with his life, his college work was only just satisfactory and he would need to improve if he didn't want to have to repeat the year. As far as Maura was concerned Sarah was doing alright. Stephen thought that Maura should give Niamh a call and try to get her to change her mind about leaving, but Maura was adamant that she didn't want her back. It would be easier without having to constantly watch everything they said and did in front of her. Maura also felt that it was probably time that she started to go out again, it would do her good; she'd get in touch with the girls and make arrangements to meet up with them soon. They were all too jittery, every time someone knocked on the front door they were afraid that it was the Gardai. Maura couldn't believe that the Gardai hadn't made the connection between Peter Dunne and her daughter. Stephen said that no one cared about a no-good drug pusher, and that he probably didn't have any friends anyway; besides, there hadn't been anything in the papers for ages. Maura wasn't so sure; she still thought that some day her daughter's name would be brought to the attention of the Gardai. When that time came the Breslin family might well fall apart, this is what she was so afraid of, and she tried to put these thoughts out of her head as she went upstairs to talk to Sean. He wasn't coping at all well and if he didn't get his act together soon he'd end up in hospital. Maura did her best to get through to him, but he didn't seem to hear what she was saying. Even now Maura wondered if they'd be better off owning up to what Sean had done; it really had been an accident.

Maura left things as they were for the time being, she would have another talk to her son the next day, to see how he felt. When she went downstairs Stephen was on the phone giving orders to the lads, his phone manner left a lot to be desired. Maura didn't tell him what she'd been thinking about a few minutes ago, he'd have thought that she was going mad. So instead she poured herself a drink, and went into the sitting room to watch the television and relax before her husband came in and spoilt that. There wasn't much of interest on the television that night so Maura switched it off just as Crime Line was coming on. The programme covered the death of a drug dealer who had died the previous October after being found lying in a pool of blood in St Stephen's Green. The Gardai were appealing for witnesses to come forward. Had Maura watched the programme, it would have helped to make up her mind regarding whether Sean should turn himself in to the Gardai. Stephen brought a drink for himself in to the room and he sat down beside his wife. He told her about his work schedule for the Saturday, he gave the impression that he was running an empire and not a small decorating business. Maura only half heard what he was saying about someone going away for the weekend; she really wasn't interested in what he was saying. Maura found it very easy to switch off from her husband's ramblings, she'd been doing this all their married life, it was the only way she could live with him. Stephen continued with his ramblings, he knew that Maura wasn't listening to him, but he didn't mind; it gave him a little pleasure to talk out loud about his achievements within the company; hiring Tom was one of these.

Maura had left the room and was getting a drink for herself. She didn't ask her husband if he'd like another one; if he did he could get it himself. She went through her phone book and checked Ciara and Holly's numbers; she planned ringing them the next day to arrange an evening out. Maura realised that she hadn't spoken to the girls for ages and she wondered what they were getting up to, and how 'Home Comforts' was doing. It was hard to believe that she hadn't even thought about her old business or the girls, she should have kept in contact with them. When she went back to the sitting room Stephen was still talking to himself, he hadn't even noticed that Maura had left the room earlier; he was hopeless. Maura sat down opposite him and just watched him for a few minutes before telling him to stop waffling. It was a nervous habit of his and was the effect that she had on him. For a short time, Stephen thought that his wife was coming to rely on him and his judgement during the crisis with Sean. However, she soon let him know that she had been in shock and now that she was over that, she was back in charge. She hadn't fully got back into checking the day-to-day running of the business, but she would go over the accounts during the coming weeks; she needed to do something useful.

Going to bed that night, Maura thought about some of the things she needed to do over the coming weeks, including totally refurbishing a few rooms in their house, her bedroom being at the top of the list. That probably meant that Maura would have to move all her personal belongings out of her room and maybe back into Stephen's for a short period of time, she wouldn't sleep in the same room but she'd use it for storage. Of course, Maura would let Stephen know about the decorating when she'd decided how many of the lads she'd need to use and when she'd need them, it's not as if she wasn't entitled to make use of their business. Being that it was Saturday the next day, the girls had probably already made arrangements for that night, so Maura decided to leave phoning them until the Monday, then they'd have time to organise a night out together or not as the case may be.

That night Maura slept well for the first time since Sarah's boyfriend had died, she didn't think it had anything to do with the alcohol that she'd consumed; after all she'd only had a few. The weekend flew by, with both Sean and Sarah appearing to have taken notice of what their father had said about pulling themselves together. Sean ate a good breakfast that morning and the cloud that seemed to be over him looked as if it had lifted a little. Maura took Sarah on a shopping trip, buying her daughter the latest fashion items and accessories; she needed to indulge her after all they'd been through. In a way it eased her conscience, she hadn't forgotten what Sarah had said about feeling so alone after her grandparents had died. On the shopping trip Maura picked up a few treats for Sean and a few necessities for Stephen, namely socks and underwear plus a cashmere sweater that was on sale; it would do him for his birthday later that year. Maura knew that if she didn't buy these things for her husband then he'd never think to buy them for himself, the poor sap, he'd never manage if he was living on his own and both he and Maura knew that. Still that wouldn't bother her too much, for years now she had kept him in everything from socks to suits. It was all down to Maura that he had anything to wear.

Chapter 16

Tom and Molly's weekend in Wicklow had been very relaxing and extremely romantic. Tom had opened up to Molly about his past and she in turn had said those three magic words 'I love you', during their romantic break. Molly had been so reluctant to say those words in case she was tempting fate by telling Tom how she felt about him, she was afraid that if he didn't feel the same way about her, that they might end up splitting up; Molly didn't think that she could bear that. Tom did feel the same way about Molly; he'd fallen in love with her. Molly was his first real adult love affair; he hadn't been this much in love since he was a teenager. He told Molly all about how he'd gone to Germany when he'd got an apprenticeship to study in the construction industry, and his consequential break up with Mo, his very first girlfriend. Molly was a really good listener and she encouraged Tom to keep talking to her. The weekend proved to be the ideal opportunity for them both to unburden themselves, and to finally put the past truly behind them. Molly thought that Tom might still have some unresolved issues to deal with, before he'd have total closure on that part of his life; there was plenty of time for that. They agreed that they were very happy with their relationship the way it was at present, and they wouldn't rush things, they were going to enjoy this time together without putting themselves under any pressure.

On their way home, Tom told Molly of his dreams of starting up his own painting and decorating business, he knew that he needed more experience in certain areas, but he was a quick learner and he enjoyed the work; he was also interested in the interior design end of the business. Tom had been lucky because he hadn't been declared bankrupt when his previous business folded, so he'd be able to start up another company if he chose to. Molly loved to hear Tom talk about his hopes and dreams, it made the thought of spending their future years together, a wonderful prospect. The weekend away had flown by and they made a promise to each other to get away together more often. Tom was going to sort out his work hours with Stephen when he went back to work on Monday. It was time that he stood up for himself, Stephen had taken advantage of him and his good nature for long enough, and Tom was more confident now, he knew that he could get another job if need be, though he would prefer to continue to work with Stephen for another while yet. There were still things that he could learn from Stephen, though not on the managerial side of the business, it was obvious that Stephen's wife was the brains behind the company and not Stephen. Tom had yet to meet Maura, but he bet his life on it that she was a bit of a witch, Stephen always appeared nervous when he talked about her.

Tom was looking forward to getting back to work; he'd spent long enough in the past without a job to go to. It was almost 9p.m. when Molly finished unpacking their bags, Tom had made a pot of tea for them, so they sat down in the kitchen and mulled over their time away. When they'd finished their tea, Tom made a few phone calls; one was to let Stephen know that he was back and would be at work in the morning. Stephen sounded gruff, he'd obviously not had such a good weekend and Tom hoped that it hadn't anything to do with him; he didn't even ask Tom if he'd enjoyed his break, he just gave Tom the address to go to in the morning. Tom was to pick up the lads as usual and Stephen warned him not to be late. The phone call had been brief, but that didn't worry Tom, he was well used to Stephen's moods.

Molly was busy with the mundane things like putting the washing machine on, and organising their stuff for the next morning, when Tom had finished his phone call. They finally got a chance to sit down together for half an hour, to unwind before going to bed. Molly asked Tom if his boss had missed him, and she laughed at the face he pulled. Tom loved her sense of humour, it was very similar to his own, they had a lot in common and Tom knew that he loved Molly and wanted to spend the rest of his life with her. They hadn't talked about marriage, it was way to early in their relationship to even think about it, but they both knew that that's where they were heading. Tom had always regretted that he had never married, but until now he'd never met the right person; Molly was the right one for him, he was sure about that. Molly couldn't believe her luck, to have found love again so soon after her husband's death was more than she deserved. Life was good.

Stephen and Maura certainly weren't feeling that life was very good for them; they seemed to drift from one crisis to another. Maura's feelings were that her and Stephen should have split up years ago, and now she knew that she'd have to stay with him for a while longer, at least until Sean had sorted himself out. That evening, Maura lost her temper with her husband, she told him to go and talk some sense into his son, Sean wasn't eating enough, he was fading away in front of them. Stephen wasn't sure what he could say to his son that would make a difference, or lift him out of his depression; but he'd give it a try. He thought that a visit to Sarah's psychologist might have a more beneficial effect than his talking to him. Maura looked at Stephen with such contempt that he went straight upstairs to talk to Sean.

He was in Sean's room for over an hour, and Maura wondered what he was saying to his son and more importantly if it would get through to him. Stephen was very quiet when he came downstairs. For several minutes Maura waited for him to speak and when he finally did, he was very vague about what they'd talked about. Maura was frustrated trying to get Stephen to tell her what had gone on and eventually she gave up and stormed out and went to bed; she didn't even go in to see how Sean and Sarah were. Maura would leave things as they were for tonight, she'd sort things out in the morning one way or another; for now she just wanted to be on her own.

Tom and Molly were up early on the Monday morning; their break seemed like a dream. They had had an early night but they didn't go to sleep straight away, they were still in a loving mood and that night their lovemaking reached a new height. Molly left for work at the same time as Tom, but she expected to be home before him; she was going to cook T-bone steaks for their dinner that night and make a side salad to go with it. Tom loved his food and he had a great appetite, luckily he never put on weight, Molly called him a thoroughbred. Tom picked up the lads and they couldn't wait to tell him that Stephen had been in a foul mood all day on the Saturday, nothing went right for him on the job. Tom said that he'd try to find out what was bothering him, but that he didn't hold out much hope that Stephen would tell him; especially if it was something personal. At work Tom didn't get a chance to talk to his boss about his problems, which were evident by his mood swings. Stephen grunted orders at the lads and Tom as well, and if anything, he was getting worse, and more unpleasant as the days wore on. Tom decided that he'd wait till Stephen had gone home, then he'd call round to his house after work, he had to try to find out what was going on, Stephen might find it easier to talk to him away from work. Tom rang Molly to let her know what he was planning to do that evening, he didn't want Molly to cook anything for him that night as he didn't know what time he would get home at. Molly didn't mind, they could have the steaks the following night. She hoped he'd get things sorted out with Stephen.

Halfway through the afternoon Stephen went off to price a couple of jobs, across town, and as soon as he was gone the atmosphere lightened and the rest of the afternoon passed quickly. Tom dropped the lads off and then headed back towards Monkstown; he wasn't sure how Stephen would react when he turned up on his doorstep. Tom was quite looking forward to meeting the harridan that his boss was married to, because Tom was sure that she must be the cause of Stephen's unhappiness. As he pulled up outside Stephen's home he wished that he'd had more time to think about what he was going to say to his boss, he really hadn't thought this through and he almost turned on his heel to leave. He hesitated for a few seconds and then he knocked on the front door. Tom could hear voices from inside and then Stephen opened the door to him. The look of surprise on his face soon changed to one of annoyance, he wasn't one bit happy that Tom had turned up at his home; any problems about work could have waited until the next day.

Reluctantly Stephen brought Tom in to the sitting room, his family were in the kitchen and almost ready to eat their dinner. Tom apologised for disturbing Stephen at home but he felt that if things didn't improve at work, well the lads were likely to walk. Tom said that if there was anything that he could do to help Stephen with whatever was bothering him, then he was more than willing to do it. He was just about to get shown the door when Maura walked in to tell Stephen that his dinner was ready, and to get rid of whoever had called at such an inconvenient time.

Tom was sitting with his back to Maura, but he recognised her voice without even seeing her, even after all these years. Slowly Tom stood up and turned to face Maura, it took a few moments for her to realise who it was that was standing in front of her. Stephen was blusteringly trying to introduce Tom and his wife, even though he realised that they appeared to know each other already. Stephen's mind went into overdrive, how did they know one another, were they having an affair? All these thoughts were going around and around in his head, but none of them made any sense, he knew that Maura hadn't gone out for ages, she couldn't be having an affair with Tom. Besides, Tom was with Molly, there had to be another explanation as to how they knew each other. As soon as Maura realised that Tom was actually her Tomas she threw her arms around his neck and smothered him with kisses. Stephen almost had to pull her off Tom, her carry on was embarrassing and at that moment she knew that she was making a show of herself. Tom was shocked to know that Maura had ended up married to Stephen, and in effect he had been working for her for the last few months.

Sean came in to see what the commotion was, and Maura

introduced him to Tom and then to her daughter, she also insisted that he join them for dinner. Tom knew that there were some serious family problems going on, and he was regretting his decision to call to Stephen's home. He found it hard to refuse Maura's invitation to dine with the family, but he was determined to make a quick getaway afterwards, the situation made him feel very uncomfortable. Maura told her children and husband that Tom had been her first and only true love, she didn't understand how offensive her words were to her husband, and everyone was beginning to feel awkward. Tom couldn't believe that she was so insensitive, and he felt sorry for Stephen, this wasn't the Maura or 'Mo' as he'd always known her. As soon as Sean and Sarah had finished eating they went up to their rooms to get away from their mother's reminiscing, she was embarrassing them. Tom, too, got up to leave, much to Maura's displeasure, but she held back from saying what was on the tip of her tongue, she knew that she'd have many more opportunities to talk to Tom; now that she'd found him again.

After Tom left Maura continued to tell Stephen about her teenage romance with 'her' Tom, all those years ago. Maura didn't notice how crestfallen Stephen was. A few minutes later Maura was left on her own in the kitchen, Stephen was embarrassed by her ramblings, and now it was his turn to walk away from her. Stephen didn't know how he'd be able to continue working with Tom after Maura's revelations about her involvement with Tom. They didn't need any more complications in their lives right now. Tom had got a shock at seeing Maura again after all these years; it was embarrassing meeting her children with the way she had carried on. He thought that she had looked after her appearance and was an attractive looking woman, on the outside, but not so nice on the inside. Tom never got to find out what was troubling Stephen, and it was unlikely that he'd ever find out now.

Tom wasn't sure how Molly would take this piece of news; she'd probably be as shocked as he was, knowing that it was his ex-girlfriend who was actually his boss. The traffic was light, as Tom drove home to Molly, he'd tried phoning her to let her know that he was on his way home, but the phone was busy. When Tom arrived home Molly was soaking in the bath, she had taken the phone off the hook, she wasn't sure what time to expect him home. Tom sat on the edge of the bath and told Molly the whole story of his visit to Stephen, and his meeting with Maura, including her overenthusiastic reception that she gave him in front of her husband. Molly was incredulous, she felt bad for Stephen and his son and daughter. 'What on earth is wrong with Maura?' asked Molly, who was unable to fathom someone like that. Tom had no explanation to offer her, he told Molly that physically Maura was in great shape, but mentally there was obviously something missing; there had to be.

That night Tom and Molly talked about whether he should continue working for Stephen, or if he should branch out on his own. They decided, together, that he wouldn't walk out on Stephen; it would leave him in the lurch and he was still grateful for being given the job in the first place. Tom would stick it out with Stephen as long as Maura didn't interfere in their lives. Molly slept easy that night, she had no worries about Tom's head being turned by Maura, Tom loved her of that she was sure. Tom wasn't as lucky getting to sleep, his mind kept going over the events of the evening, and he was pleased with Molly's reaction to what he'd told her, he didn't need her to tell him to steer clear of Maura. He couldn't get her out of his mind and he remembered the good times they'd shared when they were teenagers, they thought that they were in love back then, but they were only kids really. Tom didn't know that Maura had rushed into a relationship with Stephen partly to annoy her parents and partly as a misguided act of revenge on him.

Going to work the following morning, Tom knew he'd have to try to clear the air with Stephen, concerning Maura's declarations the previous evening. There was no sign of Stephen at work; he'd probably been caught in traffic; so Tom and the lads got started without him. Within ten minutes of starting work, Tom's mobile rang, and he wasn't surprised to hear Maura on the other end. Tom listened to her going on about the great surprise she'd had on seeing him again. Eventually she told him that Stephen was in bad form and wouldn't be at work that day, she said that she'd got his mobile number from Stephen who'd said that Tom and the lads could manage without him. Tom thought that he'd have to hang up on Maura, she was hinting that they should meet up some night, to catch up on what had been going on in their lives in the intervening years. Tom told her that she'd have to meet Molly sometime and that they could all have dinner together, Stephen included. Maura was spitting fire that Tom wasn't falling over himself to meet up with her on his own, she wasn't getting the reaction she expected, or hoped for. As for meeting Molly, that was the last thing that Maura intended doing, but she wasn't easily put off, she'd leave Tom alone for the time being, she didn't need to rush things and risk messing it up.

Tom and the lads finished the day's work in a much better atmosphere without Stephen there to moan and gripe at them.

Tom wanted to ring him about a job they were due to do next, but he was reluctant in case Maura answered the phone. When he arrived home Molly told him that he should ring his boss, he'd be expecting to hear from Tom, and he shouldn't worry about Maura. As usual Molly talked sense, so Tom rang Stephen and sorted out the query he had about work, and Stephen said he'd be at work the next day he'd just had an upset stomach, nothing to worry about. In Monkstown, Maura was behaving like a giddy teenager, and her children weren't happy with her behaviour; Stephen pretended not to notice, as usual. The talk that Stephen had had with his son was having a positive effect on him. His father had told him that he was sorry that he'd been so adamant that Sean shouldn't go to the Gardai in the beginning. Stephen now realised he was wrong, and if Sean still felt he should talk to them then he was willing to go with him. Sean said he'd think about it over the next day or two and he'd let his father know his decision. His father knew that he'd do then right thing this time and he was sorry he'd stopped him from doing so when it happened. Stephen thought that his life was just one big regret after another, he never seemed to get anything right, and now he regretted interfering in his son's life, he should have let him do the right thing from the start. It was all these regrets that had made him physically sick that day; Maura's regrets about losing Tom added to his low self-esteem. Stephen knew that his wife would pursue Tom relentlessly, regardless of the fact that he was in love with another woman; that wouldn't put Maura off, quite the opposite in fact. Stephen felt sorry for Tom and Molly because he was sure that his wife would make their lives a misery, especially if she had nothing else going on in her life. Of course Stephen was right.

Maura constantly came up with some pretext or another to phone Tom, and not just during working hours, often during the evening while he was at home with Molly; Stephen often walked in on her talking or whispering down the phone. Stephen thought that they were probably having an affair, even though Maura very seldom went out, when she did he imagined that she was meeting Tom. The next time that Maura rang Tom, Molly suggested that he meet up with her to get things sorted out once and for all, she trusted him completely. Molly wanted this over and done with before she told Tom the good news that she was pregnant; this piece of information would have to keep. Molly didn't want to share this with Tom while Maura was intruding in their private lives, and one more day wasn't going to make that much difference to her to keep this secret. Molly hugged herself, she knew that when she told Tom he'd be over the moon, he had been praying that they'd become parents, they'd talked about this for weeks now; they thought that they'd make good parents.

Maura continued to phone Tom and he was getting more and more annoyed at her, so he took Molly's advice and agreed to meet her the following evening, Tom didn't want Stephen putting two and two together and getting five.

Earlier that morning, Sean told his father that he was going to go to the Gardai and admit his involvement in Peter Dunne's death, he asked his father if he'd come with him that afternoon; of course Stephen agreed he would. They arranged to meet at the Gardai Station at 1p.m. and they weren't going to mention it to Maura until they'd done the necessary. Stephen had contacted their solicitor who would meet them there; he'd been given a brief outline of their problem and he was disappointed not to have been contacted before now. Sean was interviewed in the presence of his solicitor, and the detective dealing with the case admonished him for his tardiness in coming forward. Sarah and Maura along with Stephen would also be interviewed, and then Sean was released into the custody of his father; pending the outcome of the investigation. Sean was relieved to have finally got this off his chest, a weight had been lifted and he could now begin to have a normal life, at least until he found out what he'd be charged with. There was a possibility that he could still be charged with murder, though the detective didn't think he would, manslaughter was a much likelier charge; it would be up to the DPP once the investigation was concluded. Sean was glad that his father was with him, it had been hard reliving the events of that night over again, but in reality that's what he'd been doing ever since he'd hit the drug dealer. For now he'd have to wait and hope that the law didn't come down too hard on him.

Chapter 17

When Stephen and his son left the Garda Station, Sean went back to college as he had a lot of work to catch up on, he told his father that he'd be home for dinner that evening. Stephen thought that it was probably for the best if he told Maura what they'd done, she wasn't going to be pleased that she hadn't been included in making the decision to go to the Gardai.

Maura reacted in a completely different way to that which Stephen had expected, she was calm and she agreed that they'd handled it the right way; if she had known she might have tried to talk them out of it. Stephen was gobsmacked at this admission, Maura never ceased to amaze him.

It was late in the afternoon and so Stephen rang Tom to let him know that he wouldn't be back to work that day, he'd see him the next morning. Stephen thought he detected something odd in Tom's voice, but he wasn't sure exactly what, guilt maybe? He didn't really want to know. Secretly Maura was glad that she hadn't known what Sean had been planning to do, it was the best thing for all concerned; it would have come out sooner or later. The decision had been taken out of her hands so there was no use worrying about it now. Maura had to go shopping for a new outfit for her 'date' with Tom, and she knew exactly where to get a stunning trouser suit and all the accessories, so she headed off to town and left Stephen on his own. There wasn't much for him to do besides sitting in front of the television to watch some mindless afternoon programme. Dinner that evening was a rather tense affair, no one wanted to upset the other, so they all kept quiet. Stephen was glad when it came time to go to bed. He'd decided to go to work early the next day and then get home early in order to talk to Maura without any interruptions; he had to find out where he stood with her.

Friday was a busy day for Stephen and he got the distinct impression that Tom was avoiding being left alone with him; he was distant as Stephen tried to make small talk. Tom was uncomfortable with the situation and prayed that he'd get it sorted out that night, he was glad when Stephen finished up early; he wished that he could have done the same. Tom and Molly had talked about the likely outcome of the meeting, and Molly told Tom to be tactful with Maura if he wanted to keep his job; Tom knew that she was right. Before he'd left work that afternoon, Maura had rang him to make sure that he'd turn up that night and in the middle of the conversation she'd hung up abruptly, giving Tom no time to tell her that he couldn't stay long.

Stephen wasn't sure how long Maura had been talking on the phone; he'd only just walked in. He did know that it was Tom that she was talking to; she was using her softer, intimate voice for him. Stephen didn't know what to say to his wife, but he had to do or say something, to let her know that he was there. He coughed a little too loudly and Maura immediately hung up on Tom. 'Who was that on the phone, honeybun?' asked Stephen, trying to keep his voice level. Maura winced at the term of endearment; she absolutely loathed it and had warned Stephen a million times not to call her that, he never listened though. She hadn't heard him coming in so she didn't know whether he'd heard any, or all of her conversation, she hoped that he hadn't heard any of it.

'It was Paul,' lied Maura, 'he just wanted to catch up with me; we haven't had a good chat in ages. You're home early, anything wrong at work?' Stephen knew that Maura was lying, she'd spoken to her cousin just last week, but Stephen knew better than to confront her; he didn't want to rock the boat. He felt that if he let things settle down they might just go back to the way they'd been before, he didn't want to upset Maura, and the truth is he didn't want to know the truth. Stephen wasn't going to let her know that he knew she'd been talking to Tom so he told her that everything was fine at work. He'd come home early to try to talk to Maura, but now he couldn't find the right words so he said nothing. Maura had her back to him so he didn't see the expression of contempt on her face.

'I've made arrangements to go out tonight with the girls, like we used to ages ago. Why couldn't you have let me know that you were coming home early, wasn't there anything useful that you could have done at work?' growled Maura with more than a hint of annoyance. She hadn't meant to sound so harsh but that was how her husband made her feel now. It wasn't just because of her feelings for Tom, there were other reasons; Maura just couldn't think of them right now.

'I'm sorry hon... Maura, it's O.K. I know I should have rang you first, you're right. I've got plenty of paperwork to keep me busy, you go on and get ready, you deserve a good night out; and tell the girls I said hello.'

'I hope you're not being sarcastic, Stephen, I bloody well do deserve a night out so don't begrudge me that. Jesus,

Stephen you bloody annoy me when you start this carry on.'

'What carry on?' asked Stephen.

'This carry on, always questioning me, coming home early, trying to catch me out on something; it's as if you don't trust me, I'm sick of it,' shouted Maura, more out of frustration, than anything else.

'For God's sake Maura I don't know what you're talking about, and of course I trust you, why wouldn't I?' added Stephen.

'Forget it; you're giving me a bloody headache now. I'm sorry, I shouldn't be taking it out on you, I must be menopausal or something, sorry Stephen.'

Maura knew that she must hold her tongue, and not make Stephen suspicious; she wasn't ready to give him his marching orders, not just yet. Her solicitor had advised her to wait until he'd drawn up the paperwork before pulling the plug on their marriage. Maura was seeing the family solicitor on Monday morning by which time he'd have all the relevant divorce papers ready, and she wouldn't have to pay over a large chunk of her inheritance. It was important that Stephen didn't get wind of her plans before she'd all the loose ends tied up, Maura didn't mind this small deception, she was used to it throughout her married life.

Stephen said nothing, he looked very dejected after her outburst, and he wished that it was the menopause but he knew that that wasn't the reason. He tried to remember when it was that things had gone bad for them, he wasn't sure if it had ever been right. He knew that there had to be more to life than this, he shouldn't always have to watch what he said. He thought back to when they were first married but he couldn't be sure if they'd ever been happy. Maura was a hard book to read. When the kids had come along, things were already well and truly on a downward slope and he had left her to get on with doing the womanly things, while he got on with the business of bringing home the bacon, so to speak. Stephen always thought that this was what Maura wanted, so he didn't interfere with the way she was bringing up the children, he didn't dare to, as she was pretty hot-headed; many a dish flew past his head in the early years of their marriage, an odd one had even hit its target. Her excuse was always the same, she was either hormonal or else she said that he'd made her do it. Stephen hated confrontation, he put up with her tantrums and got on with trying to build up the business, her mood swings were best forgotten. He often wondered if this was how other married couples behaved, he doubted it, somehow he didn't think that there were many couples with a marriage like his.

Stephen wondered if he should ring Tom to see if he'd catch him out, but he didn't think that he'd be a match for him, he didn't know what to do; so he did what he always did; nothing. It was only a few weeks ago that he'd thought of firing Tom, then he remembered an old saying about keeping your friends close but your enemies closer. At first Stephen wasn't sure if he'd been imagining the cosy atmosphere between his wife and his employee, now he was almost 100% certain that they were involved. Stephen had never asked Maura about previous boyfriends and she'd never volunteered the information, they were both happy with that situation. Looking back now, they never had anything in common; if Maura hadn't got pregnant they would never have got married at all. At twenty years old her parents had insisted that they do the right thing, they didn't want their first grandchild born out of wedlock. Now he wished that they had done things their way, Maura miscarried a month after they'd tied the knot. There were too many 'ifs' and 'if only', and a lot of regrets on both sides, their marriage was doomed from the start. Stephen resented the interference from his in-laws, but he couldn't complain as Maura idolised them.

Stephen remembered back to that day five years ago, when Maura's parents were killed outright in a car crash and she went in to a deep depression, this added to the tension between them, they no longer kept up any pretence of being in love. When Maura came downstairs, she looked beautiful in a pale blue trouser suit, which Stephen couldn't remember ever having seen her wearing before; it had obviously been bought for tonight. Stephen had found a new cashmere sweater still in its bag in at the back of a cupboard, Maura obviously intended it for Tom, and she never bought him expensive clothes. Tom wore a Rolex watch, but he said that it was a good imitation, and he was always well dressed at work. Stupid, that's what Stephen thought; he'd been a bloody fool. He knew that there was no point in trying to fight for Maura; he hadn't a hope of keeping her. Stephen didn't think that his children would care; they were wrapped up in their own dramas to worry about him. As Maura went out the front door, Stephen called after her telling her to enjoy herself, and she gave a little smile that said she would. The front door slammed shut behind her, she hadn't even bothered to say goodnight, and now Stephen wondered when she would pull the plug on their marriage. He knew that she must have her reasons for not having done so already; it was only a matter of time. Stephen supposed that he should talk to his solicitor, if only to see what his rights were, he didn't know how he stood seeing as it was Maura's parents who set up the painting and decorating business for him. The in-laws had also bought them the house they were living in and Maura had come into a large inheritance when they'd died; his wife was fond of reminding him of who it was that paid the bills. Stephen couldn't help wondering how he'd fare if they split up. Oh God, he thought, surely she'd let him keep the business that he'd worked in for the last twenty-three years, she wouldn't leave him high and dry, would she? Maybe she'd want to hand it over to Tom to run, but surely she wouldn't be that cruel, would she? Stephen wondered if he could get an appointment to see his solicitor in the morning, he knew that Bob sometimes worked in the office on a Saturday morning. A sudden thought occurred to him, apart from being his solicitor, Bob was also Maura's; this could be a tricky one and Stephen knew he'd have to think about it. He felt that he already had enough problems and he didn't think he could cope with any more. Poor Stephen, he poured himself a large Hennessy brandy, which wasn't his preferred tipple, and he took a large gulp of the liquid, which went down the wrong way and started off a fit of coughing. Stephen's eyes welled up with tears, which weren't caused by the brandy, he couldn't remember the last time that he'd cried but he let the tears flow now. The rest of the brandy went down well so he poured another, and tried to decide if there was anything he could do to secure his future. After several more large drinks Stephen made his way unsteadily up to his bedroom. Maura had been using his bedroom and en suite while her own was being readied for decorating, and her perfume still filled the room. Stephen cried once more, but that night he promised never to cry again. The bedroom remained unchanged since Maura had moved out of it years ago; it was a very feminine room with lots of cushions on the bed. Stephen couldn't understand why anyone would put them on the bed in the morning only to have to remove them again that night, and repeat the process every day; that was surely a waste of time. Women, thought Stephen, they were all the same, they were never happy unless they were complaining. His father had told him that a long time ago.

Stephen rummaged in the back of his wardrobe; he knew that the gun was in there somewhere. Maura had insisted that they have a gun for protection as they often kept large amounts of money in the house. Stephen didn't want it in the house at all; but as usual Maura got her own way.

The gun had never been fired before, it had always been kept under lock and key, that is, until the kids had grown up; now it was just under some of his old working clothes, on the floor of his wardrobe. Taking the gun from under the clothes, Stephen unwrapped it from the rag that it had been covered in, and he sat down on the bed.

He wondered if he should change his clothes and put on his good grey suit. Stephen decided that it didn't matter what he wore; so he stayed as he was.

He looked around the bedroom one last time. He didn't remove the cushions; he left them where they were.

Sod the cushions.

Sod Maura.

Sod them all.